To Lizzie —

I can't live without you — please dont make me.

FOR I HAVE SINNED

※

CREA REITAN

dragon fire fantasy

For I Have Sinned

Copyright © 2023 by Amber Reitan writing as Crea Reitan

www.facebook.com/LadyCreaAuthor

Cover Copyright © 2023 Rebeca Covers

Editing by Chaotic Creatives

Alpha Readers: Lindsay H, Cassandra F, Carrie F

Beta Readers: Sarah Jane, Amanda B, Margarida T, Kirsty E

Patreon pretties: Jennifer Colleen, Rosa, Taylour, Tamara, Rachel, Suzanne, Anthia, Carrie, Cindy, Elizabeth F, Fawn, Gina, Jen B, Lauren, Megan, Nicole D, Heather F, Heather H, Miriam, Sarah, Tara, Terriann, Melissa

All Rights Reserved. No part of this publication may be reproduced, distributed, or transmitted in any form or by any means, including photocopying, recording, or other electronic or mechanical methods, without the prior written permission of the publisher, except in the case of brief quotations for review purposes.

This is a work of fiction - all characters and events portrayed in this book are fictitious. Any resemblance to actual persons, living or dead, places, or events is purely coincidental and not intended by the author.

Dragon Fire Fantasy, Inc.

dragonfirefantasy@gmail.com

ISBN: 9798877888340

ASIN:

Version 2023.09.30- P.NA

✽ Created with Vellum

Welcome to my world of romance.

This novella was originally published in the Shatter Me anthology in 2023. You will find a bonus epilogue never before released.

Please note that this is a work of fiction. What you read in the following pages is not a reflection of the author's beliefs or creed. This is a story with religious doctrine and what that can look like for those within the LGBTQ+ community.

This is a second chance romance. One of the characters suffers loss of a loved one; this is his story on how he's dealt with this. This is also a bi-awakening.

If any of this isn't what you're looking for, will bother you , or you're uninterested in these themes, please do not read. There are plenty of other books in the world for you. Otherwise, enjoy this story of finding love, sometimes for the second time, if you allow yourself to feel.

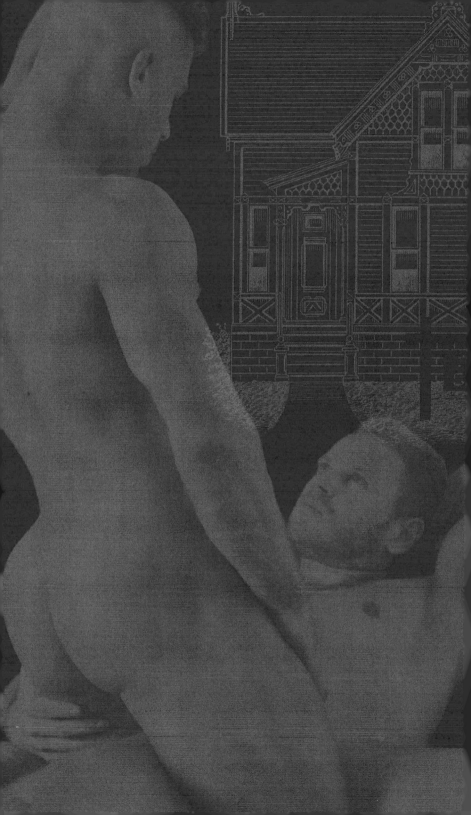

One
ZAIDEN

I THOUGHT I knew all there was to know. I'm one of those guys who's all guy. Always throwing myself into anything with my head first. I have the scars and broken bones to prove it.

The town I grew up in wasn't overly small, but it had a small-town feel with families remaining in the area for generations. Everyone knew everyone. There's a sense of pride in this town where we've kept all the old original structures intact. Not just there, closed off and condemned as nothing but a reminder, but solid and operational.

There are the old stone houses down Ringwald Way. Downtown roads are still cobblestone. The street lamps are the kind that burn with candles—except they're now electric to keep them safe. Outside the still operational old firehouse is an engine from back in the early 1900s. It still runs, and the town uses it in parades.

I went away to college right out of high school. Moved across the country to a huge city. I played soccer and graduated nameless in a sea of black robes. For the entire four years there, I felt like a nobody. Even as an athlete in a school known for its athletic department, and even as one of the better players on my team, I was still nameless. Faceless. Just a number.

Upon graduation, I came home. Most of my friends had a similar experience. There's something to be said about the grass on the other side not always being greener.

Putting my mundane business degree to good use, I became a real estate agent. It seemed like the only job that would still afford me the freedom I sought while being able to earn some decent money. Growing up, I was told I could sell anything with my smile and friendly personality. I was damn good about delivering on something impossible.

College nearly had my confidence in myself wiped out but when I got home and dropped in on my best friend Liam, also newly returned from college and feeling the same as I did, I got to talking with him and his older brother. Sam had been a realtor for years and he was attempting to talk Liam into the same career.

As I listened to them talk, snacking on his mother's famous oatmeal cookies, I thought, *this is exactly the field where I can put my skills to use.*

Six months later, I was a licensed realtor. Sam hired me. I made my first sale within two weeks. Four years later, I still work with Sam but now as a partner as opposed to just an agent. Meaning, while I continue to make my own sales, I also gain a small commission from the other agents working for our company as well.

This gives me the freedom to live. To travel. Every time I go somewhere new, I come home relieved to have gone but knowing that this is where I belong. This is home.

My next goal in life is a wife, a forever house, kids. I want it all. The only problem is that I feel like I've known everyone in my town my entire life. It's not true, of course. While we may only have one high school and not three like the big cities, we're always expanding. People come and sometimes, rarely, people go.

And yet, I'm sure that I've met everyone in my age group. A few years older and right down to just legal. Not a single woman has ever caught my interest for more than a casual dating arrangement.

Sometimes I think this is why I continue to travel. Because my wife isn't in my small town. She's somewhere else. Somewhere in the wide-open world, waiting for me to find her.

"Zaiden."

I close the app before locking my phone. I've resorted to dating apps. That's something I keep to myself. Because it's not a line of questioning I'm interested in facing.

Looking up, I find none other than Liam heading for me. I've been sitting outside my office for the past half an hour, enjoying the early summer sun. I smile as he approaches.

Liam is one of those good old boys who's all farm muscle. Which I find weird since he's only been working on a farm that neighbors our town for the past two years. Ever since he met Sofia, the pretty daughter of Danger Deer Farm. They're getting married next spring.

The idea makes me glance behind him at the soaring cathedral. Like all towns, there's a church or temple for every denomination. They range from looking like an elderly care facility to modern structures, to the old world stone and stained glass buildings like the enchanting cathedral that dominates this side of town.

I've been in it once or twice. It's fascinating. Beautiful. Haunting. I love everything about it except the doctrine that is practiced there. It's a little too... radical for me.

Liam falls onto the bench next to me. "Sofia's cousin is coming over tomorrow night for dinner. Want to meet her?"

I nod. "Yep."

Unlike most people, I don't mind being set up. Again, we're talking about my next set of goals. I need a wife first and foremost. You can't just buy a forever house meant for a future family without the other half. And since I'm convinced there's no one in town for me, I welcome whoever my friends know. Whether it be a neighbor of an out-of-town aunt or their mother's co-worker's sister's niece's twice-removed cousin's dog walker's best friend's neighbor's little sister.

I'm ready for my future. I'm not going to settle, but I clearly need to put myself out there to find her.

"Great." Liam pulls his phone out and taps away. "She's super cute. Not cute like Sofia but she's still cute."

"Mhm," I answer, knowing he's only slightly biased.

When he's finished, he looks up at me with a grin. "How many did you sell this week?"

It's Friday, so I smile because the week is over. Since I'm a partner now, I don't have to work weekends unless I choose to. That means my week is finished. "Three," I answer. "But one was a roll over from last week. The seller was being a pain in the ass, thinking their home is worth more than it is."

"Healthy commissions, yeah?"

I nod. We have that small-town feel, but we're city enough that we attract a whole lot of people looking for different walks of life. The town is ever expanding. The suburbs spilling out into the countryside, choking out farms like Sofia's family farm to make way for developments and progression.

It's a game of supply and demand. There isn't much left in the town proper, so prices are pretty high. This week alone, my commissions total almost $40,000. I mean, the houses were good sized but even the small apartments are going for more than $150,000 these days. We're talking less than 1,000 square feet. It's rough.

For buyers.

For me, it works out well. My bank account is happy.

It isn't long before more of our high school turned lifelong friends find us. James is a pre-k teacher who works down the road at the elementary school closest to my office. Nora owns a boutique shop that caters to tourists. She's been talking about expanding to make the building her store is in into an inn.

Violet is a librarian, complete with that sexy covered body look that hints at her shape and smart-ass glasses. Carter is a chef. Henry is an accountant and Wesley drives the doggy daycare bus all day. Picking up dogs and bringing them to daycare. He also does the early run for those who go home before five.

We're an eclectic group and I'm not at all surprised that we have such an array of professions. There's never a dull day and we never run out of things to talk about.

"Want to head to the courts?" Henry asks, stretching his arms over his head. He's wearing a typical button-down, but where most accountants you think of are stereotypically lanky from sitting all day staring at a computer, Henry is a little more built up because he can't sit still to save his life.

Henry has ADHD, so he's constantly restless. Thankfully, he's damn good at his job so his company has given him his own office. He's never sitting still. Always moving around. Throwing a ball at the wall as he processes spreadsheets. There's a constant input of noise so he can try to drown out all the voices in his head that pull him in eight different directions.

And when none of that works, he will call one of us until someone picks up. We stick him on speakerphone and let him ramble until he finally takes a breath, making sure that we 'uh huh' and 'yep' occasionally so he knows we're still there. He doesn't need interaction. Just an ear to listen to him until he can get all his thoughts out.

Anyway, his constant activity means he likes to run around. Chasing a ball on the basketball court is one such activity.

"Yep," Violet says, getting to her feet. "I'm going to change. I'll meet you there in half an hour."

Wesley and James join her, the three of them living in the same apartment complex. James and Violet even share an apartment.

Henry, Nora, and Carter move in the opposite direction toward their houses. We all live downtown, thanks in part to me. As the keeper of the keys, I know when something comes available first. And I can usually make sure it's affordable for my friends.

Getting to my feet, I head back inside and say goodbye to Sam and the agents who are currently at the office. Then I head out toward the cathedral. I live on the street behind it, so I'm always walking by. It's nice to live close enough to my office that I don't have to drive if I don't want to. And I rarely want to.

As I get closer, I admire the flowers and greenery. They're set up in flower beds, along paths, around benches. At first, you might not think there's rhyme or reason to how they're laid out, but as I get closer, I can see that they're very carefully planted. With exact spacing around them. Color coordinated so that they almost reflect the stained-glass windows they sit under.

It's beautiful enough that I stop to admire it. The time and dedication. Will my wife be able to master that? Hell, who's their landscaper? I want that now.

As if my thoughts were overheard, movement under the tree to my right catches my eye and I'm staring at a man. He's in black pants and a black shirt. His collar says he's a priest and yet, his hands are in the soil as he sets flowers around the tree's trunk. Moving them around until he's satisfied.

I know without asking that he's the one who planted all the plants. Did God tell him where to put them? Is that why they're so perfect where they are?

Without realizing I'm moving toward him, I come to a stop, hovering at his side. He doesn't look up at first. I get the feeling he's ignoring me, which can't be right. Priests don't ignore people.

Sighing, he leans back on his haunches and finally looks up at me.

My breath catches at his striking green eyes. I notice nothing else at first as I stare into them. I get the distinct impression he's seeing into my soul, and I squirm. Afraid of what I'll reveal. Am I overly sinful? Am I greedy?

Swallowing, I smile. Blink. And finally, take in the rest of him. His hair is short but neat. Perfectly trimmed. His face is clean shaven, revealing sharp lines and perfect lips. His lashes are long, lovely.

He's... beautiful.

"Hello," he says and everything in me stirs in a way I'm completely unfamiliar with and a little frightened by. "Do you need something?"

I shake my head. "You did the landscaping?"

He nods, his gaze scanning the yard. "I did." There's hesitance in his voice.

"It's remarkable," I say.

His brows rise a little in surprise. But what has me nearly dropping to my knees next to him is the way his lips curl. Just a little. The way it hints at true beauty if he'd actually smile.

I swallow as he says, "Thank you."

When a beat passes where neither of us speaks, he breaks the silence. "Are you new here?"

My eyes widen, and I laugh. Somehow, I find myself joining him on my knees, dropping my bag to the grass next to me. I'm close to him. Probably too close to be appropriate. I don't move. He just watches me.

"I've been here my entire life," I say. "Zaiden Nyles."

His gaze flits to the sign beyond me. The one outside our real estate office.

I nod. "Yep. I'm that Zaiden. I don't recognize you, though. Are *you* new here?"

He looks at the flowers and then at the cathedral before nodding. "I suppose. I've been here for a couple years."

"Your name? Or is it a secret?"

There's a smirk on his face when he looks my way again. I feel it in my core. Everything in me jumps. *Everything.* I nearly squirm in an effort to adjust myself.

"Ellsworth Sanna."

"Reverend?"

The smile fades, and he closes his eyes. "Something like that, yeah."

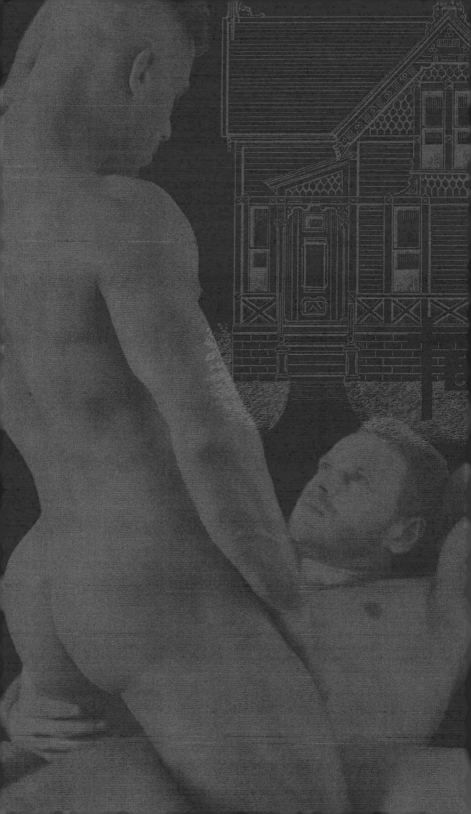

Two
ZAIDEN

I STAY with Ellsworth Sanna for the next hour. He doesn't talk much, even as he watches me out of the corner of his eye. Instead, he continues to arrange flowers. Moving them around, over and over. I'm not sure he's actually going to find the exact perfection he's aiming for today.

"Are you waiting for a sign?" I ask when he's moved the same red pot three times.

He snorts. "No." His answer is quiet. I swear, there's a bit of a bitter note in it. "I'm trying to make sense of the colors I have left."

He's got half a dozen colors. Red, purple, blue, yellow, pink, and orange. Three or four of each. "Why not a rainbow?"

Ellsworth stills, his hand hovering over a flowerpot. When he doesn't move to pick it up, I lean forward and do so, pulling it back. He follows me with his eyes this time. Those green eyes that look at me in a way that I can almost feel. Like he's touching me. Everywhere.

"A rainbow?" he asks, his voice tight.

I nod. "The elementary school kids would love that."

Tension in his shoulders releases. He glances at the cathedral again before looking at the flowers. I catch the tip of his tongue peeking out of his mouth, tracing his bottom lip, and I get distinctly uncomfortable without understanding why.

"Yeah. I could do that."

For the next few minutes, I watch as he arranges flowers again. Moving them so they're in an appropriate color wheel pattern and he sets them in a grid that's clearly a rainbow. When he takes the last one from me and sets it down, he chuckles quietly under his breath.

"They're going to think I'm flipping them off," he mutters quietly as he sits back to look at them.

"Why?"

"Rainbow?" he asks, turning his attention to me. Another hint of a smirk on his lips and *again*, I can feel it inside me. I shiver, swallow, and stare. "Are you unfamiliar with what a rainbow symbolizes in our modern civilization? What the church would love to stamp out?"

I open my mouth to answer that I have no idea what he's talking about when my phone rings and I jump. His smile widens as I nearly fall backwards over my bag in my startlement.

Reaching for my phone, I answer the call.

"Did you fall in the shower?" Liam asks.

Confusion makes my brows furrow as I turn to face the road. What would make him ask that? "What?" I scan the surrounding sidewalks, thinking maybe he's having me on.

"Where are you? You're forty-five minutes late."

Again, confusion makes me frown as my gaze slowly slides over windows of shops and residents. I shake my head. "What?" I repeat, sounding stupid even to myself.

There's muffled sounds on the other end, and then Nora's voice fills the phone. "Fuck's sake, Zaiden. We said half an hour. Not an hour and a half. Where are you? Are you okay?"

It takes me an embarrassingly long time to remember that I had plans. I cringe, sinking back on my heels. "Sorry. I... got sidetracked," I say, then glance at Ellsworth, who's arranging the rows a little more perfectly while watching me. "I'm going to skip playing ball, but I'll meet you for pizza and pool after."

She sighs in frustration. "Fine." The line goes dead. I crinkle my nose. Well, that rarely happens.

As I'm turning back to Ellsworth, I catch a flag in the window of a storefront facing the cathedral. "Ohhh," I say, turning back to face the something-like-a-reverend. "Pride flag. That's what you're talking about."

His half smile makes my stomach flip. "Yes. They'll love that. Don't you think?"

"Doesn't seem to bother you," I point out.

He looks away and sighs. "No."

Silence settles around us for a minute and I watch him. This time without pretending I'm not. I'm a quick study of people but better if they're not trying to be closed off. Ellsworth is certainly a closed book.

"When do you get off?"

His raised brow pointing in my direction makes me flush. He licks his lips and I'm horrified when my gaze tracks his tongue. Now my skin burns like I've been baking in the sun for an hour. But he likes my discomfort. The cute smile on his lips says so.

"I don't work a nine to five."

"Are you allowed free time?" I ask, hoping that didn't sound like I was being suggestive.

Ellsworth studies me for a minute. I can clearly see a debate within his hypnotic green eyes. Are priests allowed to wear contacts? They seem far too green, too captivating to be real. I'm just... enthralled by the color. So much so that I barely register it when he asks me a question.

"For what?"

I blink, once again feeling my cheeks heat. Seriously, I've never blushed so much in my life. "My friends and I are going to Strikers for pizza and pool, in a bit. Want to join us?"

He returns my stare. I determine that Ellsworth Sanna is young. Thirties at the most. His shoulders are wide under his black shirt. His biceps strain against the folded up cuffs. The buttons over his chest strain.

Biting my lip, I force my eyes not to continue trailing his body. Hello, inappropriate! Not only because I'm checking out a fucking man, but because he's a damn priest.

Taking a breath, I lean back on my heels to try to increase the distance between us. I'm sitting too close to him. That must be it.

His expression is somewhat amused now but I'm not sure which part he finds funny. That I'm clearly checking him out and horrified about it. Or that I'm basically asking him out and simultaneously want to get away from him. Maybe it's this entire situation.

"That's okay," he says, shifting his attention back to the flowers. "You don't need to invite me."

"No, I don't. But I'd like you to come." I wince at my choice of words. Especially when he chuckles quietly. I'm glad my choice of words makes him laugh. And surprised that I feel that I like being able to make him laugh.

"Would you?" he asks, not looking at me.

I sigh. "Yes. Despite me being awkward all of a sudden, I'd like you to join us for pizza and pool."

Ellsworth turns to face me, moving his body entirely in my direction, and I can see just how large he is now. The struggle to keep my eyes locked with his is enough to almost have me choking on the stress of what's building inside me. I don't recognize it and it's a little terrifying.

"Why would you like me to join you, Zaiden?" he asks. A perfectly good, reasonable question.

One I simply don't have an answer to. So I blurt, "Because I want to get to know you." And then I heat up. Again. I'm so fucking glad no one I know is around to see me fumble. I'm asking a man out! A priest!!

That's like, against their laws or some shit.

It's several minutes during which he studies me before he answers. Minutes in which my mind is turning into knots, my stomach is turning sour, my chest is getting tight. I'm so close to panic and embarrassment that my vision gets dark and I fear I might further humiliate myself by passing out.

So I'm stupidly surprised when he nods his head. "Alright."

The relieved breath that rushes out of me has him chuckling. I look up in time to catch him licking his lips again, a sexy smile on his lips.

"When?" he asks.

"Uh." I scramble for my phone and check the time. "I'll stop by in an hour to pick you up?"

His smile grows a little. "Sure. I'll see you in an hour."

He gets to his feet and I spring up to mine. Grabbing my bag, I stumble back and wave awkwardly, then basically run home.

I take a shower. Scrub everywhere. Shave and make sure I'm stupidly manscaped before pausing and staring at myself in the mirror. What. The. Actual. Fuck. Am I doing right now? Did I really just ask him on a date? Is that what he thinks? Is that even allowed? I glance down at my junk where I'm trimming my bush and cringe. Did I think I was going to take him home after?

Except, now that I've started, I can't just stop. So I finish, my entire body heated with horror at what I'm doing right now. And yet, my stomach flips with excitement. Date or not, I'm looking forward to this evening.

Ellsworth is waiting for me on a bench in jeans and a long-sleeved shirt; much the same as what I'm wearing. He gets to his feet as I approach. I stop myself from telling him I'd have gone to the door to pick him up by biting the inside of my cheek.

This isn't a date. He's a fucking priest. And that church doesn't allow gay dates!

Ah, hell, I'm not even gay! Way to leave that out of my internal reasoning.

"I don't have to go with you," he says quietly.

I look up at him and shake my head. "Sorry. I just realized how... crazy this might have sounded to you. A stranger asking you... to hang out with people you don't know."

He nods. "A little, yeah."

"Maybe I need saving?" I ask, raising a brow.

It's the first time I hear him laugh and I smile in response. Everything in me feels alive at the sound and I know that from this moment on, I will strive to hear it. And to see that smile light up his face.

I was wrong. He's not beautiful. He's fucking gorgeous. I've never seen someone so, so... perfect.

"Sure," he says. "But I'm likely going to fail at saving you."

"Oh yeah? Not your specialty?"

He snorts a chuckle. I swear, there's bitterness in the sound. "No. Not my specialty."

I nod and try not to check him out as we walk. It's not until I'm raking my eyes back up him that I realize I'm doing it. Forcing my gaze ahead of us, I silently berate myself. Since when do I check out guys? More importantly, he's a motherfucking priest! Do I need it tattooed on the inside of my eyelids so I remember that?

My friends are already at Strikers when we step inside. I lead Ellsworth to the pool table where they're gathered. James, Carter, Violet, and Henry are in the middle of a game. Liam has Sofia in his arms while they watch, her back to his chest. I find my gaze stops there for a minute as, not for the first time, I long for that kind of relationship.

But I get the strange feeling that I no longer want to be the Liam in that scenario.

Before I have a chance to freak myself out further at that thought, I take a breath and stop where they all see me. Wesley and Nora are just returning with pizzas and drinks and everyone in our little corner silences as they stare.

Ellsworth silently takes a step closer to my side. At first, I think it's so he can move behind me and out of everyone's stare. But when his hand presses *reassuringly* into my lower back, I realize it's a sign of comfort.

Giving them a wide smile, I gesture to Ellsworth. "I made a new friend. Have you met Ellsworth?"

No one answers as they stare at him. I can already see the questions racing across their faces. While none of my friends are overly subtle or anything less than blunt, I hold my breath for someone to say something.

I've known Sofia the shortest length of time. She's new to our group, only having been introduced shortly after she and Liam started dating. So I'm not surprised when it's her who speaks. She smiles, sweet and genuine, at Ellsworth.

"Hi. I'm Sofia. This is Liam."

It's her break in the silence that has everyone else introducing themselves. There's a beat after introductions are made before Wesley gestures to the pizza. "Hungry, man?"

Ellsworth nods. "Thanks."

And just like that, the game of pool continues, beers and pizza slices get passed around, and conversation ensues. I'm not sure whether I don't leave his side or Ellsworth doesn't leave mine, but throughout the evening, we remain in each other's orbit.

The only time we're parted is when he heads to the restroom

before he partners with Nora to play a game of pool against Henry and James. Liam sidles up next to me, taking a long sip of his beer as he studies my face.

When he pulls it down, I'm holding my breath for whatever it is he's going to say. "So. This is new."

I nod. "I just met him. He was planting flowers across from my office." Okay, that sounds lame even to me.

Liam raises a brow. "I see."

Sighing, I glance toward the bathrooms. "I don't know," I confess, lowering my head as I lean in and speak quietly. "I just…"

When I trail off and don't finish, Liam squeezes my shoulder. I look up to meet his eyes, scared of what I might find there. But he's smiling. "Relax, Zay. Whatever makes you happy, man. You know that."

Before I can tell him that Ellsworth is a priest and I have no idea what the hell I'm doing, Ellsworth returns. He stops at the side of the stool I'm on, close enough that his chest brushes my shoulder as he leans over and picks up his glass of water. Liam grins at me before moving away.

When he sets it down, he rests his hand on my thigh. Yep, my cock does more than twitch at his touch. I look at him and relax at the way he's smiling. It's small, but it's all for me.

"You alright?" he asks and I feel the tips of his fingers brush the hair at the base of my nape. I shiver, my cock enjoying that subtle touch just as much.

I nod. "Yes. Are you having fun?"

He looks nowhere but at me this entire time. I have his sole attention. We're in a bubble that holds just the two of us. "I am. Thanks for asking me."

"Think you'd like to hang out again sometime?" I find myself asking.

There's hesitation in his expression that hadn't been there a moment ago. He takes a breath, holds it, and eventually releases it. "There's a hundred reasons why I shouldn't," he says. There's a pause, but the inflection of the sentence makes it sound like there's a 'but.' I'm really hoping for a but.

He leans in so his lips are at my ear, his hand sliding up on my leg. I bite my tongue to hold in my groan. My eyes close as his hushed voice meets my ear, his hot breath skims my flesh. "I'm going to ignore all of them and say yes. I'd really like to hang out again."

Ellsworth backs away and I'm left biting my lip, watching as he joins my friends to play pool. I meet Liam's gaze on the opposite side of the pool table and he's grinning smugly at me. I want to roll my eyes, but they're already back on the something-like-a-priest.

My new obsession.

Three
ELLSWORTH

I NOTICE several things over the following week as Zaiden continues to come around. He isn't all about waiting outside if I'm not there. Instead, he strolls right in and has no reservations about asking for me if I wasn't in the sanctuary and he couldn't find me after a quick look around. He also never hid his grin from all the old, disapproving, prying eyes.

He invites me everywhere he and his friends go. Playing ball at the courts up on Ashbury. Back to Strikers. Or to one of their houses, usually Zaiden's, since it was pretty central to everyone's. He is easy-going, laughs readily, generous, and completely fascinated with me.

Something I picked up on early is that he is straight. He doesn't understand his attraction to me, but he clearly is not someone who is going to ignore it for the simple reason that he didn't identify as liking men. Zaiden eagerly, if not a little confusingly, embraces it.

It also makes him shy. When he realizes he is flirting or if I touch him in a way that the church *does not* approve of, his cheeks redden beautifully. It is sexy as fuck, the way his voice gets low and husky. When he stares at me with wide, willful eyes.

And each night, I go back to the church and pray for forgiveness of my sins as is expected of me. The prayers come from memory; I murmur them with my hands steepled while I kneel at the end of my bed, eyes downcast, while my mind is far from paying attention to the ingrained doctrine. The empty words.

Three years. I've not convinced myself this bullshit is real in three fucking years. But I'm still here. Still going through the motions. Pretending that I believe in the existence of a higher, divine being who forgives all.

Which I find a little hard to do. If He created all things, all men, and we're all perfect, then how can he have created gay men and shun them for being abominations? Disgusting. Unholy. It is hypocrisy at its finest. And yet, there is a loud and clear message in several passages in the Bible.

Some argue that in the original scripture it doesn't read like that. There's also an argument that anything can be interpreted however the interpreter intends it to be taken. Other denominations don't find being gay sinful.

However, the Church says that there are ways around it. You know, camps and shit that can set you straight. Pun intended.

I scoff and also refuse to give that thought substance. There's a reason I'm not a preacher and continue to just work in the Church, even after having gone through all my shit to get to this point. I don't believe in preaching something you don't believe. Not that I've ever spoken that aloud to anyone. I know that my presence wouldn't be welcome if that is the case. And I *have* to be here.

Although I also know that the priests and bishops would find it their calling from God himself to fix me. To get rid of the brainwashing. To make me 'normal' and how I was 'created.' Meaning, not gay.

The thought, even not fully formed, makes my chest tighten. Every bit of grief and sorrow surges inside me until I am almost choking. Even as I move through the day, praying when I'm supposed to—especially when I'm feeling 'weak'—and mind my own business, I'm well aware of being watched.

It took me several breathless minutes to shove it all down.

None of that matters right now. None. I finished my menial task of polishing all the fine metal sculptures and crucifixes in the sanctuary. Then, having showered and dressed, I am now waiting outside on the bench for Zaiden.

If I believe in such a thing, I know this is wrong. Sinful even.

I've given myself to this life at the Church, so I shouldn't be entertaining this. I shouldn't be seeing him every day, knowing that we're both going down a road that we shouldn't be. Or at least, I shouldn't be. However, I can also argue that if He's all forgiving, all I'd have to do is confess my sin and be forgiven.

I internally scoff and roll my eyes. It's fine. It's all fine. I'm here. I'm trying to believe. Really, I am. I try every fucking day to find a seed of truth in anything. But after three long years, I can't seem to wrap my mind around this bullshit. It feels more like brainwashing than faith. It feels empty, cult-like, and a way to manipulate the masses into falling into a cookie cutter line.

Zaiden comes around the corner, his head bowed, as he stares at his phone. I watch, transfixed at the way he moves. How his thick legs fill out his tight jeans. How his torso strains within his too-tight shirt. I can see his fucking nipples, it's so tight. He's clean shaven today and his messy hair is very clearly trying to be tamed. It's still damp, and I can already tell it's going to be a flyaway mess before long.

My fingers itch to run through it. To feel the soft, silky strands. To push his head back and watch his pupils dilate, his lips part as he stares at me. Wanting more. Afraid to ask for it.

I can see it so clearly I can almost feel it. This straight boy isn't straight at all. He just doesn't understand this new desire, having never found a man he was attracted to.

Until me.

He looks up and meets my gaze. A smile breaks out across his face. When I smile back, his cheeks flush. Fuck, I love that look on him. Flushed. Pulse racing. Breaths shallow and labored.

Sexy.

Zaiden bites his lip right before he stops at my side when I get to my feet. "Hey," he greets, stuffing his hands in his pockets. "We were thinking of going to Panta's to watch the game and eat food that will clog your arteries. Ever been?"

I shake my head. As long as I've been in this town, I haven't explored anywhere. Not until Zaiden. Even then, I couldn't care less where we are. My focus is always on him. "Nope. Let's go."

One of the things I appreciate about being here is that everything is within walking distance to the church. So I don't have to worry about having a vehicle or waiting for a ride. If I want to leave, I can. However, I'm usually too busy watching Zaiden to leave at an appropriate time. And one of us ends up walking the other home before heading home ourselves. It's been pretty evenly split.

"What game?" I ask as we stroll down the road. His hands are still stuffed in his pockets, but his shoulder bumps mine from time to time since we're walking so close.

"Soccer. Footy," he says, flashing me a beaming grin. "Then there's a rugby game on, if we're not ready to head back yet."

"There's always something to watch," I agree. In a previous life, I'd been partial to hockey myself, but I don't volunteer that information.

His group of friends is there when we arrive. Panta's is a strange bar and lounge combination. There is a bar, long and shiny and lined with liquor on the mirrored wall behind it. But there are also long, curved couches around oval tables. Each points in the direction of a large, flat screen television. It is both private and completely open to the rest of the place.

The table we head to is already covered in food and his friends are talking amongst themselves while shouting at the screen. I smile, a wistful memory long gone flitting through my mind. Of the friends I once had. Moments like this that I once partook of every week. The food we consumed and the alcohol that poured freely. Being sicker than a pregnant lady the next morning but doing it all over again the following weekend.

Loving life. My friends. My perfect home.

Zaiden's hand on my wrist pulls me from the memory as he drags me down onto the bench seating. He slides in, urging me closer until our legs are pressed together. I meet his eyes and he flushes, smiling shyly at me.

I can't help myself. I lick my lips, dropping my eyes to his. They part and I can just barely make out the tip of his tongue. I want nothing more than to taste him right now. Devour him. Instead, I drop my hand onto his thigh and turn to face the television.

"Hey, Ellsworth!" Henry says. I lean forward to look around Zaiden and offer him a smile. He pushes a plate down the table and I catch it. He grins. "Good to see you, man."

"You too," I call back, just as an uproar from a nearby table floods the room with noise.

Sitting back, I rub my thumb over Zaiden's leg, dropping my fingers to the inside of his thigh, and listening to the way his breath hitches. He looks at me out of the corner of his eye, his cheeks a pretty pink. I push the food that Henry sent my way between us. "Eat," I murmur, bringing my mouth close to his ear.

I feel his body break out in goosebumps. Zaiden scoots closer. Any closer and he'd be in my lap. But I encourage him, pushing my hand down around his inner thigh, pressing his leg close to mine. Allowing me to notice how his tight pants are being made tighter by his arousal. I am thankful mine are loose tonight. My aching dick strains uncomfortably as it is.

It has been a long time since anyone has caught my attention. A very long time. So long since I cared to even look. I am too busy being hollow and trying to force myself to believe something I don't. It's easier to say that aliens are real as far as I'm concerned. There's at least plausible evidence to support it. Unexplained things that have actually happened and are caught on film.

But there's no such thing as a miracle. Not that I've ever seen. I also find it impossible to believe that a God so powerful, so loving and forgiving, al-fucking-mighty, will allow one of his sheep to suffer so horribly before a far too goddamn early death.

Swallowing the thoughts down so they don't poison my mood, I focus back on the food in front of me. Zaiden hasn't touched anything. Too nervous. Too focused on me. So I pick up the fork and gather a bit of mac and cheese with ham on it.

"Look at me," I whisper. Zaiden turns his face my way and I bring the fork to his mouth. His lips part, eyes widening and glassy. A groan nearly breaks free from my throat as his lips cover the fork and I slowly pull it from his mouth. I watch as he chews and swallows, his Adam's apple working.

Very unholy thoughts about his throat move through my mind as I continue to feed him, sharing the fork and taking bites as well. The way he watches my mouth. The way he licks his lips. The way he turns into me, his leg coming up on mine and pushing my hand closer to his hard cock, his arm moving to rest on the back of the couch behind me. If I move my fingers even a little bit, I will feel his want for me.

I don't see any of the game. Even after we finish eating and turn forward again, his hand slips beneath the table, clutching mine. It isn't so much to keep it where it is and not explore. I think he just needs an anchor. He needs to feel me as much as I want to feel him. His hand has just slipped to my leg, daringly moving up, when Carter announces that he is calling it a night.

Most of the table follows. It is that pressure to leave too that made us stand and follow the group out. But we hang back, letting them walk ahead and put distance between us, his hand brushing mine with every step.

"Tomorrow?" he asks. "Saturday. Do you do anything on Saturday during the day? The morning?"

I do. I do a lot of things every day. Including trying to convince myself to stop giving in to this 'sinful' behavior so I can fulfill what I'm supposed to be fucking doing.

"After breakfast. Mid morning," I tell him instead of what I should. "I can meet you wherever."

"My house?" he asks, and I already know that my answer should be a resounding no. But I nod as we turn down a back street, one that's not lit as well as the others, and head for his house now. It would be far too easy to slip inside. When the world is shut down for the night and no one is watching.

We're quiet as we traverse the shortening distance until we're standing on his front porch in front of his door. He's already opened it but has left all the lights off, so we're standing in the dim glow of the moon peeking at us from behind clouds.

Zaiden steps closer, his eyes shining in the night. I swallow. His mouth opens and I quickly shake my head. "Don't ask me in," I whisper.

His mouth closes, and he nods, swallowing audibly. When he licks his lips, my moment of weakness is far too great. I pull him roughly to me and close my mouth over his. Zaiden groans immediately, pressing the entire length of his body against mine, wrapping his arms around my neck. I take far too much. Kiss him far too deeply. Biting his lip until he whimpers into my mouth.

When I pull away, I'm nearly cursing and try to catch my breath as I forcefully push down the irritating guilt inside me. I shouldn't do this. I *can't* do this.

But I don't say that. Instead, I say, "Good night, Zaiden."

He doesn't answer right away, still staring at me with wide, glossy eyes. His fingers hover over his lips. He's so fucking beautiful. So goddamn innocent and pure. So *good*. My whole body is burning with the need to bring him back against me. But I force myself to turn and walk away.

His quiet voice follows me into the still night. "Good night, El. See you tomorrow."

Fuck. Me.

I wake early in the morning and drop to my knees. It's not so much that I want to do so much as it is a force of habit. While I try to concentrate on my prayers, focusing on recapturing all the sinful shit I've been doing and asking for forgiveness, I can't ignore the bitterness in my stomach. That loud part of me that never leaves, telling me this is all garbage.

It's always loud. Always sour. Always angry that I'm wasting my life. I try like fuck to tell it off, to shove it down and keep it in its little prison, but that shit just seeps out. Like it's vapor. Unable to be contained. Unable to remain hidden and locked away. Nothing can keep it in because it's not solid. It seeps through the cracks.

My issue isn't dedication. For three years, I've done nothing but pray and study the Bible. I've listened and learned and devoted myself to this shit.

But therein lies the problem. There isn't a single part of me that believes it's more than shit. I don't care how many fucking people are out there practicing this. To me, that makes them gullible. Not faithful. Not living good, holy lives. They're going to die just like everyone else, and that's it.

I'm not sure I even believe in a soul. So the question, 'if you don't believe in heaven or hell, where do you think your soul goes when you die' means fuck all to me. No soul, so that question is invalid.

No one in my life knows that I feel this way. That I think this way. I know what it looks like to believe. How it looks to pray. What you need to portray to those watching so they think you're fully dedicated to this life.

And I know I'm good at living that lie. Since the moment I walked into the cathedral, no one has questioned me. No one.

Although, I think they're starting to since Zaiden's shown up in my life. I don't miss the looks I get, even as I outright ignore them. In fact, I *lied* when I knew I was going to be overheard, insinuating that I am teaching Zaiden the truth. Showing him the light. Saving his soul.

The words are bitter in my mouth. Not the lie of telling them, but the fact that it is *all* a lie. My life. This whole fucking construct. I knew after they left my mouth and the proper ears heard them, that their confidence in me was restored.

It makes me all the more bitter.

Climbing from my knees, I head for the small, attached shower and wash away the ick that always remains on my skin after praying. I sure as shit know that's not how you're supposed to feel. It's the same feeling I got after I touched a girl when I was trying to convince myself I was into that.

The comparison makes me chuckle and I close my eyes to the water. Getting out, I dress in jeans and a long-sleeved shirt, then push my feet into my sneakers, and leave the small bedchamber on the upper floor of the cathedral. My one request when I began this lie was that I needed to live on campus, so to speak. I wanted to be immersed.

I suppose it isn't all a lie. I needed to erase the life I was leaving behind. The life and promises that were stolen from me before I'd begun living them. If these last three years have made me believe anything, it's that I can train myself to become numb and empty. Time for prayer is really my time for meditation, when I can clear my mind from all the pain and sorrow so I can get through my day.

I leave the church and walk around the block until I'm standing in front of Zaiden's house. This isn't a good idea. Not at all. I know what's going to happen today can't be taken back. Not that any of it can be, but alone in his house, knowing that we're already pushing lines that I *can't* be?

Taking a breath, I force myself to step forward. It's been three years. I'm not going to believe in God now if I haven't thus far. Three years is a long time. Long enough that I should be able to live again. Not hide in the grief.

Knocking on the door, it swings open before I can even lower my hand. Zaiden smiles, his cheeks flushing.

"Hi," he says, stepping back to allow me in.

While I know I should be hesitant, I'm not. I'm eager. Eager to spend the day with him. To get close to him. To touch him.

In fact, I can't wait to do so. I grab his hand on my way by, squeezing it gently. He immediately returns the action and I hear his quiet sigh. The door shuts behind me as I stop. He hasn't let me go.

I look at him, and he's biting his lip. Wanting to do or say something. "What is it?" I ask.

His gaze moves to mine. A heavy, heated second stretches between us. And then he's on me, pressed against me, his mouth hot and hard against mine. The force of him launching at me has me taking a step backward to keep upright, but when Zaiden starts to pull away, mistaking the reason I stepped back, I push him against the wall. Trapping him between the hard, unforgiving surface and my body.

Zaiden groans, shifting against me so my leg is between his. His erection pressed firmly against my thigh. With his hands tangled tightly in my hair, he's given me full control of his open mouth. I'm not sure he realizes he's even done so.

He is so open to me, so pliant and eager and wanting, and I take everything I can get from him. Licking slowly into his mouth, making him chase my tongue with his. Swallowing his moans and grunts. The sounds he makes when I press my hard cock to his hip are obscene. So sexy. So hot. I kiss him harder. Deeper.

And then a loud buzzer makes him jump and I pull away, startled back into my mind. Fuck, what am I doing?

"Sorry," he whispers, panting. "I was making us brunch."

Nodding, I step back. Looking anywhere but at him, which is unfair because I can feel his uncertainty as he watches me before he moves down the hall. I take a minute to collect myself, pressing my palm to my dick to make it calm the fuck down. This isn't happening. Despite all the excitement, this isn't happening.

It can't. I've come this far.

I'm just about to yell down the hall that I need to leave when Zaiden appears again. He looks so vulnerable. So uncertain. Maybe even a little afraid. The way it pulls at my chest, I move forward, trying to offer him a reassuring smile. It's hard to do when I feel like I'm falling apart.

I close the distance between us and grab his waist, pulling his big, hard body against mine. I kiss him again, but this time, just our lips press together. "We need to slow down," I tell him, trying to catch my breath and inhale him all at the same time.

Zaiden nods. "Okay. I'm sorry. I didn't mean to attack you."

A huff of laughter escapes and I press my mouth to his to stop his ridiculous words. "Zaiden, in another life, I'd be all over this. But right now, I just—" My words trail off.

He stills beneath me before trying to pull away. His cheeks flushed. Eyes closed. But I don't let him go. "I'm sorry. I shouldn't have—"

"Don't," I tell him, my voice a growl. I press my mouth to his and while I think he's trying not to kiss me, he does. It's not fair to him. I'm giving him so many mixed signals. But I can't stop as I trail kisses over his jaw and along his neck. He whines quietly, a delicate whimper that makes me want to bite him. Finally, I get a grip on myself and just breathe in his smell. His shampoo. His soap. Whatever he sprays himself with when he gets out. It's delectable.

"What do you want me to do?" he asks, his arms hesitantly going around me.

That's a fair question and I shake my head. "I don't know, Zaiden. Just be patient with me, okay?"

"You're confused? Between your faith and... uh..."

I snort, pressing my open mouth to his neck. "Something like that," I murmur. It's all warring inside me. Not faith. Not the idea that I'm sinning and that this is wrong and *I'm wrong*. But I made a promise. And right now, everything I'm doing with Zaiden is compromising that promise.

"Something like a priest," he murmurs, and I laugh quietly.

Daring to look at him, I pull away and meet his eyes. "You know

I can't be doing this, right? In the eyes of the church, I'm committing an enormous fucking sin."

Zaiden presses his lips together. "I appreciate how careful you are with your words," he says, proving that he's always paying attention to what I say. I smile, unable to help myself. "So, let's eat before it's cold."

I nod and let him go. Zaiden moves into the kitchen and slices into the pie. When he brings it back, I see that it's not pie but quiche. I accept the plate and follow him to the booth that's set within a nook surrounded by windows, basking us in bright sunlight.

When I sit across from him, he stares at me until I chuckle and move next to him. Satisfied that I'm where he wanted me, we eat in silence until our plates are cleared. Then we sit in silence again. My fingers are tapping on the table and probably have been for several minutes when he covers them with his hand.

"Look, Ellsworth. I think I fucked up when I asked you to come with me that first evening. It's just, I've been looking for something and..." He bites his lip, staring at his empty plate. His cheeks are red as he considers his words. "And I don't know what happened," he finishes exasperatedly. "As soon as I saw you, it was like, you're who I was supposed to find." He looks at me, his eyes all wide and innocent. "Does that make me sound insane?"

I smile, my heart jumping around in my chest. Turning my hand over, I grip his in return. "No," I tell him. I know that feeling. I've felt it. Maybe more than once.

He drops his eyes. "It's not fair of me to have... made it pretty clear, I think, that I'm interested in you, given that I know that being with a man is going to send you to hell and probably get you kicked out of the church. I never thought of myself as gay. This is going to sound like some cliché rom-com but until I met you, I've never even looked at another man before. In, you know, this way." His cheeks darken until they're beyond pink and bordering red.

I grin, reaching for his face, and brush my thumb across his cheek. His eyes flutter closed for a second.

"I won't ask you to choose between your faith and exploring this with me. So while I'm going to continue to ask you to hang out, because I like your company and conversation, I'm going to let you decide what you want otherwise. Completely up to you."

"Otherwise," I repeat.

His eyes open and he's downright strawberry red now. "Physically?" he asks. "Romantically? I don't know. I did just say I've never done anything with a guy before, right? Or do you need me to say that part again? It's not like I know what I'm doing here. I'm all sorts of flustered and confused and winging it, hoping that you know what you're doing, so I don't look like an idiot."

My grin is far too wide as he's rambling. Despite myself, I lean in to kiss him, trying to put his mind at ease. "First, let me say that a relationship with a guy isn't going to be much different from one with a girl. It can get interesting in that gender roles have been leveled. It's an equal playing field in same-sex relationships."

Zaiden looks at me, his eyes widening. A smile climbing up his face. "Really? I like how that sounds. Expectations are exhausting."

I nod, chuckling, and drop the hand I had on his face. I stare at where we're still connected, our fingers entwined. "But for everything else you said? I don't know what I can give you, Zaiden. You already know that I *can't* give you anything. It's against the Church's creed. It's an abhorrent sin." I've practiced many times in the silence and solitude of my room to say those words or ones like them with a completely neutral tone. I think I even managed to pull it off.

"I hear what you're saying," he says carefully, then squeezes my hand. "But you contradict your words often, so I don't really know what to think."

"I know. That's not at all fair to you."

Silence envelopes us once more.

"What do you want?" he asks. "With me, in case that wasn't clear."

I chuckle and shake my head. "That's the problem, Zaiden. What I want and what I can do are two entirely different things. But I'm not sure which one I'm strong enough to follow through with."

"Is one harder than the other?" he asks.

"For different reasons, yeah. They're both steep mountains. I'm not sure which one I'm going to be able to ascend." I look at him, hoping he sees the sincerity in my eyes. "I don't want to hurt you or give you hope that I can be what you need or mess with you. *I don't want to hurt you."* I emphasize the last words. "But I don't want to stop seeing you either. Even if this is only going to be a mess."

Zaiden nods. He holds my eyes for several minutes during which I think he can see as much moving through my gaze as I do his. Finally, he leans in and kisses me softly. Just presses his mouth to mine and stays there. Not a proper kiss. No movement. We're just feeling each other. Letting our lips mold together. Become familiar. Breathe each other in.

When he speaks, he doesn't back away so I can feel his lips move against my mouth. "Then I think you still have to call the shots," he says quietly. "I've never had this consuming draw, this overwhelming *need,* for someone before. So, as messy and hard as it might get, I'm not going anywhere. But I won't kiss you again. I won't touch you again after this. That's going to be on you."

I grumble at his words. He's right to do that. But fuck, I can't be trusted with that. I'm going to hurt someone and it's likely going to be both of us!

"Just know that I want you, Ellsworth. So fucking bad," he says, his voice low, deep, needy.

Everything in me groans as I lean into him again, but I don't kiss him. Just keep our mouths together. This is going to have to be enough for right now. Because I can't leave the Church. I can't. I made a promise that I'm just not willing to break. The thought of breaking that promise is far too painful.

But fucking hell, I don't know if I can *not* do this with Zaiden. He's right. Sometimes when you meet someone, you just know. And I fucking know this man is going to wreck me.

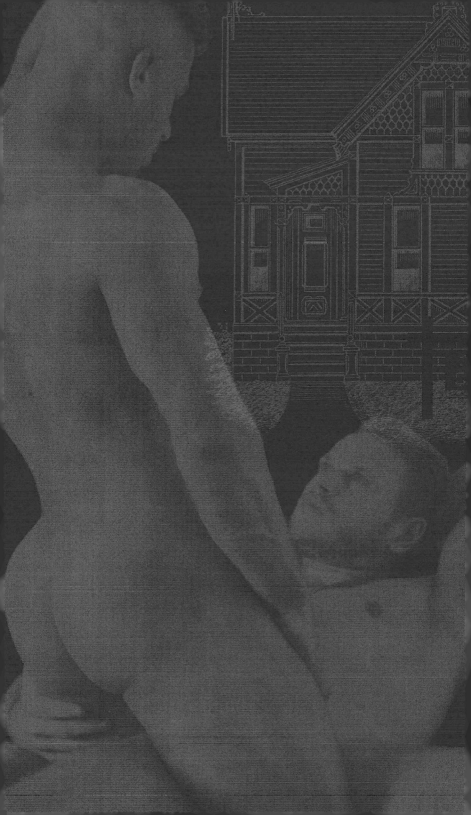

Five
ZAIDEN

THE NEXT FEW weeks are a hell storm of confusion for me. I'm a hot fucking mess with how Ellsworth comes and goes from my life. I can't even be mad about it. He warned me. He told me in as many words that he *can't* do this.

And I know he can't. I really do. And it's awful of me to have put him in that position. But fuck if I can stay away. I need him in the worst fucking way.

The need is so consuming I feel lost and absent most of the time when I'm not with him. My skin is tight. I'm so goddamn horny. And terrified of being so, because anything with Ellsworth is terrifyingly new.

Not that we've done any of that. He's kissed me a handful of times since that Saturday that we laid it all out. But I can physically see the turmoil in his face when he does. If that's not enough, it's the pain that follows. The pain that's bright in his eyes.

It's not regret. I don't see that. But I'm sure his fight is much worse than anything I'm going through. He's dedicated his life to the Church. And in that life, being gay is reprehensible. Unclean and one of the ugliest sins.

The pressure I've put on him is disgustingly unfair.

But no matter how many times I tell myself that, I can't stay away. I can't.

After that Saturday, I didn't see him on Sunday or Monday. I even stopped by the cathedral, hoping he'd be outside. When he wasn't, I went in looking for him. He wasn't in the sanctuary or any other place open to the public. I asked about him and was told he wasn't available.

Fuck, did that hurt.

But then he was here the next day at my door, and I nearly sobbed in relief. I threw myself at him, only horrified and embarrassed after the fact, but he hugged me just as tightly as I clung to him.

"I'm sorry," I muttered. "I know I shouldn't be putting this pressure on you."

"Hush," he whispered, his arms getting tighter still, his fingers digging into me. "I came here of my own free will, Zaiden."

And that's the push and pull we've been playing for three weeks. I try to be okay with it. Trying not to let it hurt. Remind myself I had no fucking business hitting on a priest. None. I did this to both of us. What kind of person am I to give him that kind of temptation, knowing he can't get involved with me without being shunned from his fucking life?!

My only bright spots are when he shows up. Because I know he wants me. It's a reminder that he does. A promise that he's suffering as much as I am. And while I don't want him to hurt like this, I appreciate that I'm not alone. That this isn't one-sided.

No matter how many times I warn myself that I shouldn't fall for this man, I do a little more every time I see him. With every touch, every stolen kiss, every smile. Every time we speak about something silly or casual or just sit in silence, I imagine myself growing old with him.

But I come down off that high real quick when I remind myself that he's a man of God and when it comes down to it, those men choose their faith first. Not someone they barely know. The reminder makes me sick. Brings tears to my eyes. Everything in my body hurts as I curl up at night and pray with all my fucking might that he chooses me.

The version of God I believe in doesn't have any issues with followers being gay.

The three weeks of back-and-forth lead into this week where I haven't seen him at all. Not once. I've been to his Church so many times looking for him. Begging for him. But those fucking miserable old crones just look at me with disgust and tell me that Ellsworth isn't taking visitors.

There's a dark fear in my gut that says he was found out and forced to leave. That he's not really there at all. That those assholes are purposefully not telling me that because they're dicks and believe that I'm broken. Or that they think keeping me from him will fix me.

Really, it's just breaking me more.

I don't know what to do with myself as I stand in the stupidly tall double doors and stare into the sanctuary. It's peaceful as my blurry eyes track down the center aisle between the pews to the pulpit straight ahead. The vast stained-glass windows paint the space an ethereal rainbow of colors. There are glass chandeliers hanging from the arches in the stone ceiling. Medieval-looking sconces on the wall. The stone floor is polished smooth from so many feet moving about.

There are doors all over the place. In the little entryway where I stand, there's one to either side. At the end of the room, behind the dais are two more, leading back and away. Right inside the sanctuary doors are other sets of doors on either side with stairs behind them, heading to the choir decks that overlook the sanctuary.

There's a small dais at the front to the right where a beautiful pipe organ is sitting. It's old and grand, something magical in itself. Opposite that are the confession closets. I don't care what they're actually called, they're fucking closets as far as I'm concerned. And I scoff at the idea of confessing.

There's a priest sitting in one of the front pews, looking at me, his eyes all squinty. Unkind. Judgmental. I don't even glare back. I let my heartache and pain shine brightly in this room that's supposed to be filled with all things good.

Finally, I turn away and walk out. Aimlessly moving through town. Not knowing where to go. Not knowing what to do. Who to talk to.

I tried telling Liam what was going on, but I couldn't bring myself to get the words out. I wasn't ready for anyone to commiserate with me. Besides, telling someone about this thing with Ellsworth will bring on more questions than I'm prepared to deal with. Maybe if Ellsworth and I were in a better place, then I could face them. Liam would help me. I know he would.

But that's not the case. And my chest fucking hurts. It's been six days since I've seen Ellsworth. Something around six weeks since I first saw him planting flowers. I've never hurt so much in my life. Nothing has ever left me this raw. This broken and lost.

I wander for hours. Not seeing or hearing anything as I make my way up and down streets. Not stopping to eat or drink. It isn't until I find myself at my office and let myself in that I feel how very worn out I am.

My office has a small fridge that I keep stocked with water for clients. I drink two bottles before collapsing on the couch. I can't go home. I don't have the energy to do that. To be alone. He's been there many times and everywhere I look is a reminder that he's not there now.

Even my fucking room, where Ellsworth hasn't been, is a reminder. Because it's there that I've researched what gay sex means. What it's like. What it looks like and sounds like and feels like. All because I *have* to be with this man. There's no other option for me.

But what the fuck am I going to do if he's already made his choice?

I told him that he held all the cards, and I wouldn't push. But did I tell him I'd accept his decision if that decision wasn't me? If I was a better man, I would. But I'm not. And I won't accept it.

That doesn't answer what I'm supposed to do right now. Wait for him? What if he never comes? What if I never see him again? How am I going to go through life with this gaping hole in my heart? My chest hurts like I'm having a heart attack. I'm sick to my stomach. My head is constantly pounding with a headache that just won't go away.

Closing my eyes, I lean back and focus on my breathing. Trying to clear my head as the silence of the office surrounds me. I've been shit at my job this last month. I know Sam's getting concerned, but I don't have anything to tell him. Nothing to explain that I feel like I can say out loud.

This is my misery right now. My burden to carry. My heartache to suffer alone.

I must have dozed. When I open my eyes, the office is dark. Sitting up, I scrub my hand over my face. I feel raw. Everything inside of me feels raw.

Forcing myself to grab another water, I drink. Then I head home and shower, washing away all the day's gross feelings and wishing it would disappear down the drain. Wishing I could step out of the shower and Ellsworth would be there waiting for me.

But when I get out, I'm alone. My house is so silent it grates on me. I dress numbly, tears stinging my eyes. When I stand in my room, I fall apart. Every determined stubbornness I put in place when giving Ellsworth all the cards fell away.

"I can't do this," I said and stuffed my feet into my socks and shoes. Not caring at all if I look like a fucking homeless man, all fucking rumpled and facial hair so long it looks like I don't have access to a razor, I practically run down the sidewalk in the dark.

Run around the corner and sprint to the fucking church. I tear open the door and pause, looking around. It's quiet. Just the sounds of a slumbering church.

Only once, Ellsworth mentioned that he lived at the cathedral. That meant his room was here somewhere and fuck if I wasn't going to find it. With a 50/50 chance, I choose a door and try it. Expecting to find it locked, I'm elated when it opens and relieved when it does so silently.

The hallway is dark. I give my eyes a minute to adjust and creep along, peeking my head in every door that's unlocked. My heart is racing when I don't find him on the first floor.

Finding the stairs, I climb as silently as I can, freezing every time they creak or groan under me. My heart is in my throat as I stare, knowing that if someone comes out at any sound, I have nowhere to hide. There is no good reason for me to be back here. None at all. My mind is too much of a scrambled mess to even come up with a good lie.

Not that a lie would convince anyone. Everyone would know I was here to find Ellsworth.

By some fucking miracle, I make it upstairs and stare at the doors that line the hall. The first few are open, and I peek in, already knowing that he's not going to be in the room with one of the open doors. By the time I get to the one I'm convinced is his,

I'm a sweaty mess. Terrified. Ready to burst into tears like I'm three years old and skinned my knee after falling off my bike.

I stare at the door, knowing that he's there. Praying that he's there. Finally, I gather the courage to knock.

I'm shaking now. Can barely breathe. I'm a fucking wreck as the light flicks on and reaches my feet from under the door.

Tears sting my eyes when I hear the knob turn. And then it opens, and I look at the man I've fallen in love with. That I have no business loving. A tear falls down my cheek as I look at him, just as much a mess as I am.

I don't find any comfort in that. Not this time.

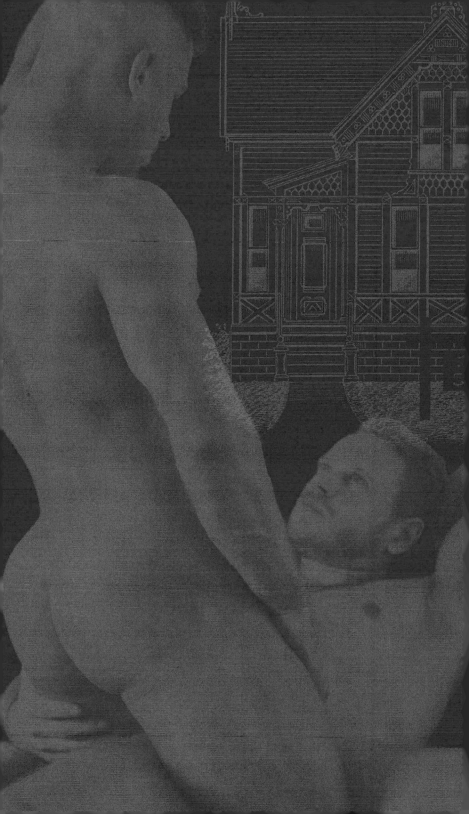

Six
ZAIDEN

"Zaiden," he whispers, his voice strained. His eyes travel all over me and his face falls, reflecting the pain I feel. "What are you doing here?"

I don't have any words. Instead, I blink, unleashing more tears.

Ellsworth makes a sound and reaches for me, grabbing my shirt and pulling me into his room. I don't have time to look around as I wrap myself in him. His door shuts quietly and then I'm pressed against it as he holds me tight.

Although I know I'm trembling, I think he is too. Where it had once made me feel better knowing that he hurt as much as I did, right now I just want it to go away. I want something I can't have. And I'm here to beg for it.

First I need to catch my breath.

He lets me pull away, but before I can speak, his mouth is on mine. Kissing me with such desperate abandon, I know he hasn't been hiding from me easily. I can taste his pain. Feel how much he wants me. How his need burns as hotly as mine does. I can feel the holes in his heart as if they're my own.

They are mine. We share those holes.

I pull my lips from his and say, "I need you, Ellsworth. I'm sorry, I know I said—"

He doesn't let me continue as he kisses me again. I need to tell him, though. I need—

When his hands find my stomach under my shirt, the thoughts leave completely. This is what I need. His hands on me. His skin on mine. I frantically pull at his shirt, needing more. We stumble about in the small space as we strip each other. It's a needy, feverish mess of wild touching, tasting, memorizing every inch of skin revealed.

Naked, Ellsworth has me on his bed as he climbs on top of me, kissing me deeply. I'm ready for him. Ready for him to touch me. To make me his in every way. I fucking *need* everything about this man to complete me. To heal me.

His mouth travels down my body, licking and biting as I writhe underneath him. "Ellsworth," I quietly beg, knowing that I need to keep my voice down. No one can know I'm here.

"I know," he says, licking up the length of my shaft and making me gasp as I clutch his hair. When my fingers tangle in it, I realize it's not as short as it usually is. My mind swirls with that thought mixed with the feel of his tongue on my dick. The feel of his scruffy face on my balls.

And then I'm in his mouth and I buck up without meaning to. I try to apologize, but he sucks in the most expert way. I'm so fucking desperate for him that my balls are already drawing up tight.

But he doesn't stay there long. Releasing my cock, he moves lower, sucking my left testicle into his mouth. A whimper escapes me. He lets it go, telling me, "Shh. You have to be silent."

I nod frantically. But when his lips land on my taint and keep going lower, I have to pull a pillow over my mouth. The gasp I let out when his tongue rings my hole is indecent. Loud. Guttural. I'm almost chanting his name.

He stops and pulls the pillow from me, his mouth landing on mine before I can beg him to keep touching me. "I don't have anything in here. It's not allowed," he says against my mouth.

"Spit," I say. "Make it work."

He smiles against my mouth, resting his body on top of mine for a minute and just holding me. I hug him tightly as he tucks his face into my neck.

"Please, don't let this be it," I whisper. "I'll do whatever you want, El. Anything. I can't do this without you."

I feel him swallow. "Can't do what without me?" he asks, his mouth at my ear.

"Life. I can't live without you. Please don't make me."

The sound he makes cuts through me. It's sharp and pained. Filled with so much tangled emotion. He kisses me again, shaking his head. I don't know if that's an agreement or him telling me he can't promise that. He kisses me for a long time, slowly rubbing his cock against mine.

While I'm frantic under him, he's slow. Steady. As if he knows what he's doing.

Going down my body, he resumes licking at my hole. Ellsworth alternates between his tongue and pressing his finger against me. Pressing at my tight ring. Quietly murmuring for me to relax and that he promises he'll make it good for me.

I need to tell him that there's no fucking way in hell I'll be able to keep an orgasm with him quiet. There's just not. Nothing about what I feel for this man is quiet. It's loud and needy and determined to be heard and seen. No matter how I try to keep it tucked away while he works through his own hurdles.

His finger finally pushes past my asshole, and I groan long and low. He chuckles, his tongue still lapping at my hole, making sure I'm well lubed. "That's it," he murmurs. "Let me feel inside you."

I do. I feel him so fucking deeply and yet I know he's only barely in my ass. His tongue touches me, making me moan, pant, and wiggle with impatience. I pull at my dick, trying to give it a little relief where it begs for attention against my stomach.

It's not long before I realize Ellsworth knows what the fuck he's doing. He alternates between sticking his tongue in my ass as far as he can, which makes me howl into the pillow, and shoving his fingers in there, fucking me with them. Making me feel things I didn't know existed. Pleasure I had never experienced.

He's so thorough, so careful and meticulous at what he's doing, that I barely realize he's stretching me as he's toying with my ass. Pushing his fingers in and just teasing at the pleasure that I know is going to tear through me. It feels so good that I'm unconsciously pressing into his fingers. Needing more. When I actually begin begging for it, he pulls back and climbs up my body again.

There's a distant thought that he shouldn't kiss me. He's had his tongue in my ass, for fuck's sake. But that thought is silenced when his mouth is on mine. It's hot and delicious, the way he takes me and brands me from the inside.

"Want to get my dick ready?" he asks into my mouth.

My face heats. "I don't know how."

He smiles. "Just need your mouth, Zay. Open for me and get me wet."

I shudder at his words, so fucking eager to taste him. I nod. At his chuckle, I realize it is a little wild. He kisses me again quickly before crawling up my body.

His dick is... magnificent. Who knew I'd ever think that about a dick? He hovers over me, his dick in his hand, hard, swollen, and red. Angry for attention that he hasn't been giving it. My mouth waters.

"Open," he murmurs.

I do. As wide as I can. And it slides in. I moan around him, the salty taste of him making me almost hysterically turned on. I need something in my ass. His fingers. How can he shift around and stick them back there? I need both.

"That's it," Ellsworth whispers. "Don't need to suck right now, love. Just get me wet so I can slide inside you."

A moan, loud and fucking needy, fills his room. I know it's mine. Even with his cock deep in my mouth, I'm loud.

His eyes are molten above me, staring at me. "You like this?"

I nod frantically. So fucking much. Hasn't he figured it out yet? This is it for me. Everything about him makes me messy and untamed. Wild.

He shoves his dick in a little further and I gag, my hips rising off the bed. Ellsworth grunts. "Alright. Fuck, that's enough or I'm going to lose it down your throat."

Reluctantly, I let him go, licking my lips when he pulls free. His mouth comes down on me again, hard and hot as he slides down my body, positioning himself between my legs. I grip his hair. "You're so eager," he whispers, pressing his lips all over my face. Kissing my cheeks, my eyelids, my jaw, everywhere.

"I haven't ever wanted someone like I do you. I'm yours. Just take me, El. Please. I'm ready."

He groans, reaching one of his hands down between us. Finally, I feel his dick at my entrance. He pushes gently, wasting no time. I'm fucking scared out of my mind and glue my mouth to his.

His pushing pauses as he kisses me until I calm down. "Easy, love." My heart soars. "I'm not going to hurt you. Raw is going to be a little more uncomfortable than it should be, but I won't hurt you. Promise."

I nod. "I need you inside me."

Ellsworth leans his forehead against mine, sighing. I know, right then, that he's thinking that he shouldn't be doing this. It's so loud in his head that I can hear it. I swallow hard, gently rocking my hips up, pressing against his cockhead.

He licks his lips. Inhales deeply. "I haven't done this in so long," he whispers. "Haven't even thought about it."

Reaching up, I kiss him softly. "Please," I whisper back.

Adjusting our position, he gently pushes against me again. I try to remain relaxed because I don't want him to change his mind. When his cockhead breaches me, I grunt, blink my eyes several times as if that's going to push away the foreign feeling. The sting. The uncomfortable stretch.

I liked his fingers in my ass. Why is this so different?

He releases his cock and takes my hand, lacing our fingers together. His breathing is as heavy as mine is while he gently rocks his hips, moving deeper and deeper inside me by fractions. I know he's getting there. I can feel the way my body stretches. Burns and makes room for him.

But even my fucking ass knows what's up. Knows that this man is it for me. And he's going to be in my ass every fucking day if I can help it.

"Am I hurting you?" he whispers.

I shake my head. "No. It's just... weird."

His chuckle makes me smile. "It'll get better," he says. "Tell me if it's too much. You don't need to take all of me."

I snort. "Like fuck I don't."

Ellsworth picks his head up and grins down at me. That look. That smile. It makes my chest expand with warmth. Does he know I love him? That I'd give up everything to be with him? Is it the wrong time to tell him right now?

What am I thinking? Of course, it's the wrong time. He has his dick in my ass. I'm delirious.

Too distracted by what I'm feeling for him, I don't notice when he's already balls deep. I don't realize that I'm moaning as he gently moves in and out of me. It's not until he hits the magic spot inside me that can only be my prostate that I'm slammed back into reality and shout.

He cuts it off with his mouth over mine. From that moment on, that's where his mouth remains as he makes me feel so fucking good, I'm flying. Wild. On fire. My orgasm builds so full that I'm bursting. But it just stays there. Defying gravity and making me mad, insane.

Ellsworth's body against mine is everything. He never lets go of my hand, gripping it tightly as he kisses me senseless, swallowing every sound I make. Every dirty, indecent, sinful sound as he takes my body and owns it. Molding it to fit his. To please us both.

When my orgasm finally finds me, I'm in freefall as I cry out into his mouth. My ass clenches as it fills with new hot liquid. I'm only slightly aware that he's come in my ass, filling me with his seed. Marking my soul as his own.

He can have it. I'm his until the day I die.

And then we collapse. For a minute, we don't move. His mouth is still pressed to mine, keeping me silent and unable to fully take a breath. When he finally looks down at me, I can see the questions in his eyes.

Is this okay? Are you okay?

"I love you," I blurt in a whisper. Then wince at the words that left my mouth. Fuck. What's wrong with me?!

His breath leaves him. Emotions race in his eyes before he takes a breath and kisses me again. Softly. Gently. Filled with words he can't say but tries to make me feel, anyway.

And then he shifts to pull out.

I break our kiss. "No," I say quickly, clenching my ass around his cock. "Stay there. Please."

A smile climbs his lips. "You want me in your ass while you sleep?" he asks.

My heart flutters because he just said, without saying, that I'm sleeping here. I nod, desperately. "I don't want to be separate bodies yet," I say, feeling my cheeks heat at how foolish that sounds.

His face softens, and he presses a kiss to my lips again. "Okay." He lets go of my hand and wraps both his arms around me, tucked under me, holding me tight so I'm pressed between his body and the mattress. His hips curl up, keeping his cock wedged inside me, even as it softens. "Sleep, love. Feel my heart against yours."

Tears prick my eyes for the hundredth time today. I hold him tightly, the hand in his hair I can't convince to loosen even though I know I must be hurting him. He just holds me tighter in response.

My heart hammers against his until it beats at the same rhythm. My ass throbs, knowing that his dick shouldn't still be there, but I love every weird ache and strain. His arms are like a vise around me. His breath on my skin is a reminder that he's here and alive and with me.

Tomorrow is going to be scary. Because I know we're going to have to talk about this. But right now, I finally have everything I want. So I go to sleep, not letting these tears fall. Even they need to remain just where they are. A part of this perfect moment.

Seven
ELLSWORTH

I WAKE with a start but feel weighed down. Disoriented. A groan leaves my throat and I try to shift. It's only then that I feel the body under me and last night comes racing back.

Oh fuck. What did I do? I already know before I shift enough to look at Zaiden sleeping peacefully under me. He said he loved me last night. The ache in my chest that never really leaves pulses hard. I glance at the simple dresser across the room, at the cross that sits there. The bottom half is part of a frame while the top half grows out of it. There's nothing in the frame. Just the generic picture that came with it.

It's a landscape. Beautiful. Suggesting that everything is happy if you have God in your heart. All that rubbish. You know it well. We all do. I scoff quietly and turn back to the sleeping man beneath me.

My dick softened enough that it slipped out of him while we slept. I winced. Fuck. No condom either. Not like I had one here. I have nothing here. I'm a man of God. This is a goddam sin! An unforgivable sin.

A sarcastic voice inside me says, *until you confess and all your sins are forgiven.*

But it's not just that. I glance at the cross again, but my gaze lands on the clock. I've only slept for a few hours. It's nearing four. I release a breath of relief and turn back to Zaiden. He needs to leave.

He *can't* be seen here. Not at this time of night. And sure as fuck not coming out of my room!

"Zaiden," I whisper, pressing my cheek to his and my lips to his ear. He murmurs nonsense in his sleep and a smile finds its way to my lips unbidden. "Zaiden. Wake up, baby. You need to leave."

"No," he whimpers, turning his face into my neck. His arms tighten around me. "Please, I can't—"

"Shh," I tell him, brushing my mouth over his. "You can't be found here. I need you to understand that. You have to leave."

"But—" He blinks up at me, the upset and hurt shining in his glassy eyes as they fill with tears.

"It's okay," I tell him, my heart slamming in my chest. There's nothing okay about this. Nothing at all. "Go home and I promise I'll come over right after mass. First thing. I'll be there. I promise."

His chest is heaving, but he nods. We get out of bed, and I do my best to clean him. At least a little. He's got dried cum everywhere. I ignore the way it fills me with heat again. Ignore the way my cock grows hard at the sight.

Once we're both covered, I peek into the hall and hurry him out. Checking at every door for someone. We meet no one. When we're standing outside, he turns to me, a clear desperate plea in his eyes.

I kiss him quickly. "Go home, Zay. I'll be there in a few hours. I swear. Go home and wait for me."

Swallowing audibly, he nods. I watch him turn and walk down the path. When he gets to the sidewalk, he looks at me. And then he runs home.

I turn back inside and stare blankly. What did I do? Fucking hell, what did I just do?

Returning to my room, I shower and change. Then I drop to the floor at the foot of my bed and silently fall into prayer, letting my mind slip into meditation as my lips form the familiar, practiced, empty words.

The bells call me out of the calm and quiet state some time later and I'm down in the sanctuary where I move through the motions of mass mindlessly. My gaze is far off. My thoughts are a stir of pain and panic.

When it's over, I follow the small crowd of people through the door. I don't take a left on the sidewalk but a right. Following the back way around the cathedral to get to Zaiden's house. Hiding what I'm doing. I don't even change. Or tell anyone I'm going anywhere. I just leave. Let my feet take me to the man I *can't* want.

His door opens right as I raise my hand to knock. He looks like a wreck. His face is blotchy, like he's been crying. The relief on his face when he sees me is so filled with emotion that my stomach flips.

I'm through his door then, pulling him into my arms and kissing him hard. Deep. We stumble against the door as he climbs me like a tree, wrapping his body around me.

"Please," he says into my mouth.

"What do you need?" I ask, biting at his lips as he moans, his hips thrusting against mine. His cock is hard, straining.

"You. Please. I just need to feel you again."

"You must be sore," I say. I can't. I can't. I can't.

"Ellsworth," he says, the crack in his voice makes me move into his house. I know where his room is. I've been here enough times to know. Though I've never been inside.

The door is open, and I bring us right to the bed. We fumble with our clothes. Tearing them away, impatient when we have to stop for buttons or the way the material resists being pulled free. Finally naked, I'm on him, rubbing against him as he greedily touches me everywhere.

"Lube," I say.

He nods, gesturing for the drawer in the nightstand. I move up him, feeling his mouth on my chest and stomach. He just barely reaches the head of my dick as I grip the drawer handle. I grunt as he slurps, his hands gripping my ass cheeks as he tries to get more. For a minute, with lube in my hand, I let him. Let him taste and explore.

But I can't stay like this. I'm as starving to be in his body as he is for me to be there. Last night wasn't anywhere near enough. Last night was strained, forced to be slow and quiet. We don't have that issue here.

I cover my fingers in lube and press them to his ass. Zaiden immediately lifts his legs higher, but his mouth comes off me as I push two inside.

"I don't want to do this part," he gasps, his hips bucking. "Just your cock, El. Fuck me. Make love to me. I don't care what you do, but I need your dick inside me."

My mouth covers his as I shove a third finger in, just as impatient as he is. I kiss away his protest, silencing him and swallowing all the delicious sounds he makes. Far sooner than I should, I pull away and get more lube, covering my dick.

And then I'm there, covering his body and pressing back inside him. He doesn't hold back as he cries out. His heels press into my ass cheeks, begging me to go deeper. So I do. I push inside him until I can't go anymore, though I seriously wish I could. I want to be in his chest. In his lungs. In his mouth. Everywhere.

I still for a minute, letting us both catch our breaths. When he looks at me with feral eyes, I get to my knees, grip his wrists, and fuck him until he's a wild animal beneath me. I don't hold back, though I should. He's new to this. New to something in his ass.

But I don't. I can't. Not when every sound he makes spurs me on. Encourages me to fuck him harder. Demands me to get as deep as I can. His ankles land on my shoulders on either side of my head, and I barrel into him until he comes with a sob, spraying his body as if he was a water pistol. The stream is ropey but strong, shot with a force so hard that it covers up his neck, the pillow under his head. Lands in his hair.

When he's limp, completely pliable in my arms and moaning dazedly, I curl him in half and empty in his ass. Fill him with every fucking drop of seed I have until it's leaking out around my dick. Then I still, gasping for air, and fall next to him.

He whines when my cock falls out. "Nooo," he tries to pull me back, but he's too tired.

I pull him against me with my noodley muscles and try to shove my half hard dick in his ass. It's not quite successful, but it's enough that he stops whining.

Zaiden sighs and dozes in my arms as I watch him. He looks peaceful. Happy. A smile stays on his lips.

My thoughts start to creep back in, but I try like hell to keep the bubble of peace. It's flimsy but I manage. Manage to remain still and just watch him breathe.

Then suddenly his eyes snap open, and he blinks before looking at me. His ass clenches and I grunt, feeling it around the head of my cock, since that's all that's still in his tight hole. Zaiden smiles. "I need you there," he murmurs.

I dip my face, kissing his shoulder.

"Don't tell me this can't happen again," he whispers.

The words don't leave my mouth. Not because they're untrue, but because I know that I'm not strong enough to stay away. I close my eyes as the conflict rages inside me.

"Ellsworth?"

"Yeah?"

When he doesn't answer, I look up. He's got his lip between his teeth. Worry shining brightly in his eyes.

"I'll figure this out," I tell him quietly. "You need to be patient, okay?"

"You're not going to hide in there again, are you?"

I rest my forehead against his. "I'm sorry, Zay. So sorry. I didn't mean to hurt you. I just—I needed to..."

"I know you're hurting too," he says. "And that what I've asked of you isn't fair. It's shit. I'm so selfish. But I can't do what I said. I can't wait for you to choose because if I do, you're going to choose God and I can't live with that."

I scowl because the concept of God has nothing to do with my turmoil. But I don't say that. I bite the inside of my cheek and try to figure out how to explain this. The war inside me. Why I really shouldn't do this. Why it hurts so badly that I do.

Words don't come.

OVER THE FOLLOWING WEEKS, no matter how many times I try to tell him why I can't keep doing this, the words don't come. Because it feels too good. Not just sex; though sex with Zaiden is the only thing I've ever experienced in my life that makes me believe that there might be a heaven. But all the quiet moments too.

Our conversations. His laughter. The way he looks at me. How vulnerable he is, opening himself up and giving me everything. Everything about Zaiden Nyles threatens to undo me. To my very core, I'm tangling around him a little more every minute.

The only thing I made him promise was that he not come back to the cathedral at night. He can't be there. Not like that. I can't risk it.

He doesn't. Instead, I quickly finish up whatever menial task I have to perform, say my mind washing prayer, and run away. Then I disappear inside Zaiden's house, into his body, for days at a time, only returning when the moon is out. That way, I don't see the disapproving faces. I don't have to hear the voices in my head admonish me. I'm too tired to feel the dull throb in my chest and the way my stomach churns, knowing I'm fucking up everything. That I'm breaking the last promise that I ever made to the only person I loved with my entire being.

Eight
ELLSWORTH

When I'm not with Zaiden, I'm numb. Empty. I welcome it because it means I can keep losing myself in everything Zaiden. I let that easiness, the feeling of him and the way he wraps around me make me feel again.

Not a lot. I can't afford to feel too much. But just enough. Just enough to remember that I'm alive. But when I look in the mirror, I don't see myself. I don't see anyone I recognize. The man's eyes are tired with no vitality in them. His shoulders are slack. And his face is a mess of unshaven growth.

I turn away because I can't bring myself to focus on the face that stares back at me.

If only you could see what I've turned into. I don't think you'd be proud.

Blinking away the thoughts that make my chest tight, I open the bathroom door just as Zaiden steps back into the bedroom. He's carrying a tray and warmth bleeds into me as he grins.

So happy. So full of energy and love to give. And he's chosen me to give all that to.

Guilt rushes through me, and I have to swallow it away.

"Sit," he tells me.

I do as he says and sit on the bed, my back against the headboard. He looks at me for a minute before changing his mind. "Scoot forward, El."

Watching as he sets the tray on the bed beside my legs, he

climbs in behind me and then pulls my back to his chest. He sighs as he wraps around me, peppering kisses all over the side of my head.

I let his touch, his affection, his clear desire for me wash away everything that I feel when I'm alone. Even when we're only separated by a bathroom door. That's all the time in my head without him I can stand. It's enough to send me spiraling.

"You smell so good," he whispers.

Grinning, I let my hands fall over the one he's got resting on my chest. Over my heart. "It's your body wash and shampoo," I tell him.

"You make it smell different. I could get lost in you. Just like this."

Sighing, I close my eyes, relaxing completely into his embrace. For a while longer, he continues to rub his nose against me, breathing me in deeply, hugging me to him as he kisses every bit of me he can reach in this position.

"Open your mouth," he whispers.

I do, without bothering to open my eyes. A fork lands on my tongue and I close around it, taking the food he's offering me and tasting the sweet, fluffy pancake overtake my tastebuds. I hum in appreciation for how good it is.

"Carter taught me the secret to five-star pancakes," he says. Over the last several weeks, he's told me more and more about his friends. I know them all by name, their occupations, where they live, how they met. All things I hadn't learned when we hung out because that was just for fun. Not an opportunity to get to know each other.

These details were important to Zaiden, though. How he knew his friends. How important they were to him. And he wanted me to be a part of that.

Since we started sleeping together, I haven't seen his friends. It's just been the two of us sneaking around. Mostly, I come here. But in a few weak moments over the last week, I've had Zaiden in my room.

There's something about having him in my bed. Forcing him to be quiet as I stuff him full of my cock.

I shouldn't feel this way. Or do this at all, never mind in the fucking cathedral. I don't know why I do. But I can already anticipate when I'm in that mood because I ask him to come. Once, I kept him well into the morning where I fucked him mindless and numb on my bed while mass was happening in the sanctuary. If it wasn't for the volume of the organ and the fact that every priest and other member of the Church was in mass, we'd have been caught. Zaiden wasn't quiet, and I didn't try to muffle him.

It was self-destructive. I snuck him out shortly after. After cleaning him (which consisted of me licking his cum off of him) and making sure he didn't leave a trail of my cum on his way out, I let the numbness settle inside me.

Numbing away the guilt. The fear. The pain.

The anger at this whole stupid establishment. Still, I fell to my knees in my room at the edge of my bed. My bed that was covered in both our cum and sweat. In my small room, where I could still hear his cries of pleasure echo off the bare walls. I could still feel his touch on my skin.

On my knees, my mouth mindlessly repeated some prayer of penance as I let the hollow words bring peace to my head. Clear the thoughts. Let my body enter into a state of meditation.

But that didn't last long. As soon as mass was over, I left the Church and headed straight for Zaiden, where I fucked him again on his bed. And now he's feeding me breakfast.

He sighs happily behind me. I smile, knowing I make him feel that way. But my smile fades because I know this can't keep happening. This isn't the kind of relationship he deserves. To be with a fake man of God who can't give him anything real. I can't let anyone know. This is all hidden behind closed doors. It's a secret and will always remain that way.

Zaiden must know that. He's a smart man. But if he does, he doesn't say anything. He never brings it up.

I try to. Often. But I don't try too hard because I know when I finally say something, that's going to be the end of this. And neither of us is ready for that.

It's going to hurt and I'm not ready to deal with that kind of pain. For either of us.

THAT DAY COMES SOONER than I thought it might, though. I'm becoming too reckless. Doing things like inviting him to sneak into the Church, we hook up there wherever I can sneak him in. I'm trying like hell to convince myself it's because I need him too badly to keep my hands off him. But I think we both know there's something else twisted in my mind that's driving this need.

Zaiden doesn't question me. He comes when I ask him to and he gives me his body to please wherever I push him to hide. He's quiet, learning to contain his shouts of pleasure. His whines and his moans and every other seductive noise he makes.

But I can see the question in his eyes when I tell him to meet me at the Cathedral and where. When. He knows I'm spiraling. He knows I'm losing my grip. There's worry in his gaze but he nods, giving me what I desire.

I'm waiting for him to show up today. Waiting in the shadows of the main floor, just inside one of the doors at the back of the pulpit, where I have a clear view of the doors outside. Waiting to see him.

My dick is already straining. Aching. I palm it impatiently, cursing myself for letting my body get this out of control. That's why I'm so insistent on Zaiden coming to me. So I can let my body have its moment of weakness and then continue to dedicate my life to this bullshit.

That's why. That's what this is about.

Abomination.

I scowl as the word echoes in my head. Movement in the sanctuary catches my attention and my eyes dart right. Father Dallon is cleaning the dais. Slowly, methodically running a cloth over it. I know it's damp with holy water and then followed with oil.

Trying not to roll my eyes, I turn back to the door and my heart jumps. Zaiden is standing just inside, looking around warily. I lick my lips and realize he's uncomfortable with this. He glances up at the cross and sighs as he slinks away.

Stepping back further, I wait for him. Staring into the dim hall, I see nothing until I see him. He smiles immediately, but I can't erase the look of wariness I just witnessed from my mind.

"Hi," he whispers, coming straight into my arms.

I hold him tightly, feeling my feet hang over the edge of a well.

Knowing I'm about to fall. I won't be able to pull myself back up. Once I fall, I'm gone. Drowning.

"Hi," I whisper in return. For a minute, I do nothing but hold him to me.

Then my body can't take the way it's burning from the inside. I pull him back and we stumble into a closet. From past experiences, I know the door doesn't latch completely. There's no lock. "You ready?" I ask in his ear as I lick at his exposed skin.

Zaiden nods. He grabs my face and kisses me hard. Greedy. Desperate. The same way he always kisses me. There's something else there too. Something new. It hurts to taste and feel, but I'm not sure what it is.

He turns, bracing his hands on the wall as I shove his pants down. And then mine follow. With his pants around his thighs, he can't spread his legs as wide as usual, so when I push my dick between his cheeks, he's already gripping me hard.

His body tenses in anticipation. Shakes with need. I reach around to grip his dick and realize it's still covered. Lifting his shirt, I find he's wearing a jockstrap, giving me full access to his ass while containing his cock.

A growl low in my throat makes me press my chest into his back.

"You like it?" he asks shyly.

I nod, pushing the head of my cock to his tight, lubed hole. He certainly is prepared for me. Came well slicked and ready. "So damn sexy," I growl in his ear.

"I thought it would contain my mess a little," he said and then gasps before he can stop himself as I breach his hole.

The strangled, choked noises he tries to keep in have my blood boiling as I slide into his tight ass. I groan quietly, burying my face in his hair and breathe him in deeply. I grip him tightly, one hand around his chest and the other squeezing his dick through the thin fabric.

"You feel so fucking good," I mutter. Giving neither of us time to adjust much, I begin fucking him steadily. I'm enjoying the sounds he's making, even with his fist in his mouth as he tries to stifle the noise. But he's too loud today. Too needy. I just had him less than twelve hours ago, but he's still so fucking horny for me.

It isn't long before he almost shouts with his release. The thrill of being caught brings my release to the front. I'm just about there as the door to the closet bursts open. We're deeply hidden in the back behind long robes and a box that hides our legs.

Zaiden stills as I shove my dick deep in his ass and hold my breath as I come hard. The priest's eyes lock into the darkness, but he doesn't see me. His penetrating stare searches, but he doesn't see.

Cum continues to pulse out of me as my knees shake and my vision darkens around the edges while I continue to hold my breath. I'm dizzy. I'm going to fall.

The priest leaves and I let out a breath, slumping my body weight against Zaiden.

The thrill of being caught, yet not being seen, is making me high. But it also scares the fuck out of me. I've been playing with fire and I just touched it.

As much as I fucking hate everything this building stands for, I can't let it be taken from me. I can't. I will hate myself if I break the promise I made. The thought stings my eyes and my stomach churns.

I shouldn't feel like this after sex. I should feel good. Like I always do with Zaiden. But the knowledge that I'm going to break a promise that I can't bear to break is my undoing.

In silence, we pull up our pants. I know Zaiden must be stupidly uncomfortable with my cum dripping down his leg and his underwear trapping his around his dick and stomach. Swallowing bile, I silently sneak him out a side door.

He looks at me, and as soon as our eyes meet, he knows. Zaiden shakes his head, reaching for me, tears already bright in his eyes. "Don't," he pleads quietly. "Please, don't do that."

Biting the inside of my cheek hard enough to draw blood, I don't hide the turmoil from my face. I let him see it all, including the tears that are building. Reaching for his hand, I grip him tightly. "You're everything," I whisper, letting him hear the strain in my voice. The way it cracks. "Please know that."

Then I back away and shut myself inside. And my world comes crashing down around me.

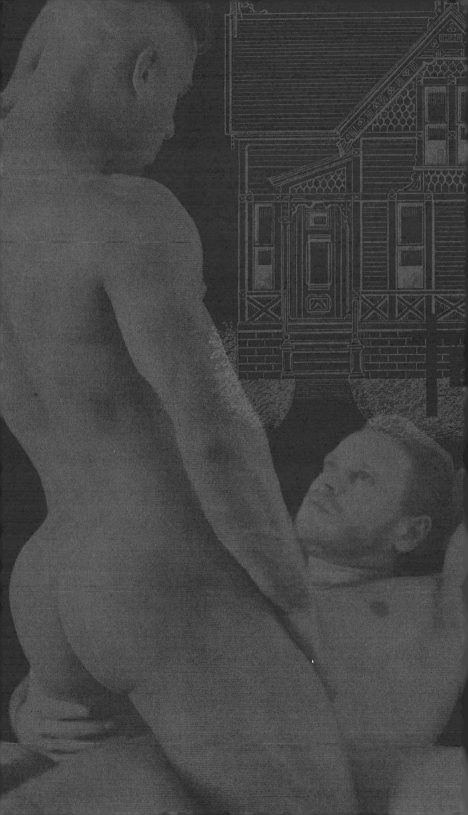

Nine
ZAIDEN

I STARE at the door for a long time as tears sting my eyes but refuse to fall. He's going to come back, right? He has to. I told him I can't do this without him. I told him. I thought he understood.

Even as I saw the signs coming for days now, I ignored them because I thought this was what he needed. He needed me in his house of prayer. He needed to know that I could share the space with him. I could give him what he needed, regardless of where we were.

I'd been ignoring the part of me that screamed in warning. Telling me that this wasn't a good idea. Not just because it was disrespectful, but because I could see the way it was eating at him.

Like Ellsworth was trying to hurt himself.

I stand there for a long time, still unconvinced that he is going to just leave me there. The door opens at one point, and I throw myself at him. But the man, the priest who caught me, isn't Ellsworth.

He looks at me with pity, but I'm positive it isn't because he knows what I am upset about. What broke me.

"Would you like to come in, child? Pray with me? Confess?" he asks gently.

I shake my head. His God wouldn't help me. He'd likely strike me dead for wanting to be with a man. For coming all over the walls in his Church.

It was then that I force myself away, telling myself that he just needs time. He'll be back. He'll come back. Because he understands that I can't live without him. That he's the reason I live and breathe. He loves me. I know he does. Even if he didn't say the words to me, *I can feel them.* I know.

But the days pass, and Ellsworth doesn't come. I go to the Church and look for him every day. When I ask, they no longer say he's unavailable. Now they tell me he's not seeing people.

He won't see me because he knows he won't be able to stay away. That's what I need. I need to see him.

But the doors to the back halls are locked at night now. There's no way to get to him.

So instead, I sit on the floor in my living room and stare down the hall at my front door. Waiting for him to come back. Waiting for him to remember that we belong together. Willing his love for me to win.

I'm staring through tears and don't see the door open. I don't hear the person coming toward me enough to recognize them. All I know is that it's not Ellsworth. How will I live without him? He can't expect me to.

How will he live without me?

"Zaiden."

I know the voice and I lean into the touch when Liam places his hands on my face.

"Fucking hell, look at you, Zay." His voice is gentle and though he must be close if he's touching me, I can't see his face through my tears.

"What happened?" he asks. I feel him close. Feel his legs against mine. His hands are still on my face, rubbing my cheeks softly. "Zaiden, tell me what happened."

"I pushed too hard," I whisper. The words spoken out loud tear a sob from my chest. Misery coats my entire being. My chest aches like something is sitting on me, crushing my ribs, my lungs, my heart. They're going to snap and pierce my lungs.

"You need a vacation?" he asks gently.

What is he asking? I shake my head. A vacation won't help. Shaking my head dislodges my tears and I can't stop the trembling now.

Liam swears and pulls me to him, causing me to tumble and fall into his chest. He wraps me awkwardly in his arms as I cry. I'm grateful for his affection; I need to be seen right now. To not be alone. But I couldn't bring myself to tell anyone, or say it out loud. It wasn't allowed to be said.

This was Ellsworth's life on the line. Not his actual life, but his life in the Church. His eternal life. I couldn't take that away from him. And yet, I desperately wanted him to choose me.

"Tell me," Liam says gently.

I hiccup and take big gulps of air as he holds me at a weird angle where we're both using far too much effort to remain upright.

"Does this have to do with Ellsworth?" he asks softly.

Biting my lip, I try not to answer. But I think not denying the question tells him that it does. His hand pats my head, brushing down my hair.

"What happened, Zay?"

"I want him to choose me," I whisper. "It's not fair because I know he can't, but I want him to." It all comes tumbling out at that point. How I found him in the flowers outside the cathedral. Then how I kept asking him to hang out, and he did. Even how I kissed him, and he told me he couldn't do this.

How I kept going back when he'd try to pull away.

How I snuck into his room, and we had sex in the church. The weeks following. The weeks of pleasure and happiness.

I tell Liam how I fell in love with him.

All the way up to what happened days ago. Now I'm alone. I know he wants me. I *know* he does. But how can he believe in something that says he can't be with the person he loves? I need him to love me enough to come for me. To choose me over his faith.

"It's not fair of me to ask. I shouldn't expect it. It's not fair of me to want it, but I do," I say through my gasps. "Tell me how to make that happen. I'll do anything."

Liam's rocking me now. Holding me tightly to his chest, still in this strange and awkward angle. He continues to pat my hair. But he says nothing.

I don't blame him. There's nothing to say.

Minutes go by and I get my tears under control. I'm just leaning on him now, listening to the steady rhythm of his heart.

"Listen, Zaiden," he says gently and I can already tell I'm not going to like what he has to say. "It sounds like you've made your intentions with him clear. I don't think you have any choice but to wait for him and see if he makes the right decision."

"I can't," I whine pathetically. "What if he doesn't make the right decision?"

Liam chuckles. "Zay, what you consider the right decision and what the right decision for him is, are two different things."

I pull back and glare at him. "You said that I should wait for him to make the right decision. What decision did you mean?"

His smile is sympathetic as he brings his hand back to my face. I don't like that look. He's not going to say what I want him to.

I need him to tell me that Ellsworth will come back. He'll choose me. But the way Liam is looking at me says he doesn't believe that to be the case at all.

"I meant the right decision for him, Zaiden," he says. His words sting. Tears burn my eyes again, and I try to look away. "I'm sorry. But if he's not letting you see him, I think maybe… he might have made a decision."

"No!" I demand. "I don't accept that! I won't."

"What are you going to do?"

There are so many things I want to say that I'll do. And I'd do them all. But I already know I can't follow through. Ellsworth wouldn't appreciate them for the gestures that they'd be meant as. Everything I'd do would tear his world apart.

Then he'd hate me. He'd resent me, at the very least. I don't want him to be with me as a second choice when I've made his first choice for him. Against his will. Even if he'd be with me after that, when I've forced him out of the Church because I was selfish and fell in love with something-like-a-priest when I shouldn't have, he'd not be there because he wanted to be. Because *he'd* made the decision.

He'd be there because I stole the life he chose from him and now he had to live one that he didn't choose.

"Nothing," I whisper. The defeat in my voice stings. It makes everything in me hurt.

Liam gives me another sad smile. "Come here." He pulls me to him, and we end up laying on the floor with my face in his chest. "I know you can't see this now, but everything will be okay. I promise. Even if you don't get the outcome you want at this moment, that doesn't mean it's not the way it's supposed to be."

"Are you saying God doesn't want us together? Because right now, I don't give a fuck what he wants."

Liam chuckles. "You know I don't believe in God, Zay. But that doesn't mean I don't believe there's somewhere in life we're supposed to end up. That certain people are meant to be in our lives. Maybe it's hard to see right now because it hurts too much, but this might be a necessary stepping stone for you to get where you need to be."

"How so?"

"Well, before Ellsworth, you've never considered the possibility of being with a man, right?"

I didn't like where this was going.

"Maybe you needed him in your life to show you that men are an option. You've been searching for your next goal, Zay. A wife. So you can have your forever home with a wife, kids, and a picket fence. The whole works. But maybe you were never supposed to have a wife. Maybe you're supposed to have a husband."

I sigh in irritation. "Yes. Ellsworth."

"You're awfully stubborn," he says, chuckling.

While I don't disagree, I also don't agree with his reasoning. I won't. I know what I feel. And I know that if Ellsworth chooses the Church over me, I'm not going to love another person. Not like this. Not even if I do what Liam is suggesting and move on. Find someone else—be it a wife or a husband—I will never love them like I do Ellsworth.

And is that really worth it? Is it fair to me or this future Mrs/Mr. Nyles? They'll never have what they should have from me. Because it will always be Ellsworth's.

Liam sighs. His fingers move through my hair as he hugs me to him. He's never hugged me before, but I guess I've never needed it.

"Thank you for being here," I whisper. "Even if I refuse to believe you."

He chuckles. "You should have called me, Zay. I want you to know that you don't ever have to go through anything alone. You're my best friend, fucker. I need to know when you're hurting so I can be here for you."

"You found me," I argue.

"Yes. Because no one has heard from or seen you in weeks. You haven't answered your fucking phone. My brother says you haven't been to work."

I wince and scowl. "Yeah. Hopefully, I still have a job."

"Sam will understand," Liam assures me. "But for fuck's sake, Zaiden. Don't shut me out. Not when you need me here."

I nod.

"I'm not going to push you to move on or forget him. But I'm also not going to let you shut yourself in your house and waste away. Understand?"

"I'm not much company."

"You don't need to be anything other than what you are. Happy. Sad. Miserable. Combative. I don't care. You aren't doing this alone."

I press my face into his chest and let my tears run over. Just one more time. Because I can. Because he's going to hug me, and I won't be alone for a little while. I'll allow myself to take comfort in that. For just a minute.

Even knowing when I open my eyes, Ellsworth still won't be here.

Ten
ELLSWORTH

It's been a long time since I felt this kind of ache in my chest. The all-consuming pain that leaves you breathless and miserable. The kind that prevents you from taking a full breath, no matter how hard you try. Like someone's lying on your chest. Squeezing your heart until it's nearly a pancake.

Making you feel like you're having a heart attack. I'd shut the pain out for years. Three years. I've made it go away, carefully constructing the numb shell around me, emptying my mind of anything—memories, pain, guilt. And filling it with the bullshit that helps me forget.

Because that bullshit just irritates the fuck out of me. All the lies that the fucking Church preaches. Their contradictory and hypocritical doctrines. It just fuels a never-ending fire of anger inside of me that people are so fucking gullible to believe it. Following it like fucking cattle.

Sheep. Docile and mindless. I get the flock thing now. It's fitting.

Taking a breath, I try for perhaps the dozenth time over the last several days to push it all away. But no matter what I do, it refuses to go back into its hole. I can't get the pain to go away. I can't convince my body to stop reacting as if I was experiencing the devastating loss all over again.

It's worse this time. Because I never dealt with it the first time, and now it's happening again.

A clink and crash startle me and I suck in a breath as I turn my head to look at my dresser. I've been laying on my bed for days. Have I even gotten up for anything besides to piss? Probably not. Others have come in with water and bland food, convinced I've come down with food poisoning.

That would be a welcome ailment, so I could stop feeling so fucking much.

My gaze flits tiredly over my dresser. There's not much there. A lamp. A Bible. The cross frame that I brought with me as my one possession.

As I look, my eye catches on the fact that it's the cross that fell over. The frame came apart, which shouldn't have been possible. Behind the cross is the picture that I keep close. The only picture I have of the life that was stolen from me.

New tears sting my eyes as I stare at my face and the man I lost three years ago.

Struggling to pull in another breath, I sit up and stare. It shouldn't have come apart. That damn frame was glued together. Because I couldn't go without that picture, but I obviously couldn't leave it behind. He's the reason I'm here. The only reason I'm here. It was his belief, not mine.

Getting to my feet, I cross the room and touch it. A tear trickles down my face and I suddenly feel a weight lifting.

I can't do this.

Stripping from my clothes, I get into the shower and wash away the multiple days' worth of misery. And sweat, tears, pain. Everything. Only the sweat really washes away, though.

When I get out, I somehow shave while refusing to look at myself in the mirror. I have to do something. I can't keep doing this. This is no way to live.

Dressing, I pick up the picture and pocket it before leaving my room. Leaving the church. I head down the street, heading for Zaiden's house. I stand in the middle of the walkway, staring at the door for several minutes as I try to compose myself.

Deep breath. It's time to come clean. Time to admit defeat and everything else I've kept to myself.

Licking my lips, I walk to the door and knock before I can convince myself otherwise. There's noise and a minute later, the door opens. It's not Zaiden.

Henry looks at me with a brow raised. His gaze looks me up and down before he frowns. I probably look like a fucking mess.

"There's a priest here for you, Zay," Henry calls, but doesn't move away from the door. He doesn't let me in. He protects his friend.

Dread slips over me as the thought that maybe Zaiden doesn't want to see me runs through my mind. A new throbbing pain cuts through my chest and I scratch at it, trying to ease it away.

Over Henry's shoulder, down the hall in the living room, I see Zaiden. He looks like a wreck. Like he's been sick. His hair is all over the place, and his face is covered in many days worth of growth. His eyes are glossy and sad. I swallow as our eyes meet and I can feel his pain, knowing I did that to him.

He moves toward me, almost hesitantly. When he steps past Henry to stand on the threshold, I falter for a second longer before I reach for him and pull him to me, crushing my mouth to his. He sucks in a breath before his arms wrap around me, clinging to me tightly.

Catcalls behind him make us pull apart. Zaiden glances over his shoulder before pushing me outside and closing the door. Then his arms wrap around his middle protectively as he looks at me warily.

I don't blame him. I've done nothing but hurt him. Probably since the day we met, I've done nothing but hurt him. I should have stayed at the Church. But I couldn't.

Reaching into my pocket, I pull out the picture. Looking at it makes everything in me ache as a tsunami of grief overtakes me. With a shaking hand, I give it to him.

I watch his face as he studies it, bringing it closer to look at the two men. Tears sting my eyes and it takes everything in me not to let them fall.

"That's you," Zaiden says.

I nod.

"And this is?"

"My husband," I whisper, making him look up at me in surprise. "My late husband."

Zaiden swallows as he studies my face. His eyes are glassy with his own unshed tears. Taking a breath, I let it out slowly, trying to clear my head of the need to cry.

"Just over three years ago, I lived with my husband. Our life was... well, I can look back and say it was perfect because he was here and alive. We had our fights, our challenges, but I loved him with everything in me."

I have to stop for a minute as tears suddenly well up and I can feel my face crumple. It's a struggle to keep from sobbing, so I hold my breath, not giving the sobs any fuel. It takes far too long to contain them, and when I speak again, my voice is shaking.

"I was away, visiting family. He had to stay home. There was a project at work that he was desperate to get through so he could relax. The plan was that he'd meet me in a couple days. The day he drove out, he called me from the road. He was so excited that he finished early and he was coming to join us. Only ten minutes after we hung up the phone, it rang again. This time with a police officer telling me my husband has been in an accident."

There's no stopping the tears this time. Probably because I see Zaiden's start falling. His shoulders shake as he tries to contain his sobs. His arms tighten around himself as he listens.

"I'm not sure how I got to the hospital." I'm not sure my voice is comprehensible right now as I try to get the words out. This is a story I've never repeated since the moment it happened. "He was still alive when I got there, but barely. We got to say goodbye."

I close my eyes, remembering how he looked all banged up and filled with tubes. Machines beeping unsteadily. Then too, I tried like hell not to cry because I wanted to look at him clearly. I wanted to see his face and remember it always. I tried desperately to burn his face into my mind. Behind my eyelids so I'd always see him when he was no longer there.

"He told me he loved me and that he'd never leave me. He promised he'd always be here, but that I couldn't just shut down. And he made me promise that I'd live." I choke and have to stop for a second, my chest rising and falling as I desperately try to breathe. It feels like that moment all over again. The pain and helplessness feel the same. The grief is crippling.

"He asked me to do him one favor. My husband was a spiritual man. I... I was not. I *am* not. But he asked me to find God. To make peace. For him, I promised I would."

Zaiden shakes his head. He wipes his face as he looks at me.

"After his funeral, I took this photo and left it all. I swore that the only thing I was going to do for the rest of my life was work to find his fucking God. Imagine how difficult and frustrating that is when I don't believe in this shit!" I laugh bitterly, shaking my head again. "How can I when *He* says that being gay is a sin? That I'm fucked up and broken. I'm an abomination. In one breath, these fucking priests say that God made us all perfect. And in the next, I'm condemned to hell for being attracted to boys instead of girls."

He tilts his head a little as he watches me. It takes me several breaths to finally quiet the quaking turmoil inside me. To quiet the heartbreak and grief that's moving around inside me like a hurricane, threatening to pull me under.

After several breaths, I look down at the picture.

"But it was the last thing he asked of me. And if that's what he wanted, then I was going to give that to him. I made that promise and have been trying to fulfill it, but it's... not really happening."

"I'm sorry," Zaiden says.

I shake my head. He reaches out and presses his palm to my chest. "You've never dealt with your grief, have you?"

Another bitter laugh escapes. "No," I whisper. "I used this fucked up Church to silence everything inside me so I wouldn't have to feel it. It worked to some extent. I use their tedious mind washing prayers as a way of meditating. Using the familiar words as background noise to clear my head."

Zaiden laughs. "That's not how you're supposed to use prayer."

I smile a little and nod, stepping into his touch a little more. I need the pressure against my chest. His touch, it's the first time since my husband that I actually feel anything at all.

"I'm sorry," Zaiden says again. "I didn't mean to... disrupt what you had going on."

I laugh without humor. "Yeah. It's fine. It's not like I've been living the dream."

I'm not sure I was living at all.

Eleven
ELLSWORTH

A QUIET MINUTE PASSES. I cover Zaiden's hand over my heart with my own and close my eyes. Again, I feel lighter. Another weight has been lifted. Was it from acknowledging my grief? Allowing myself to think about my husband? Maybe it was just explaining my actions to Zaiden.

"Can I show you something?" Zaiden asks.

I look up to meet his eyes and nod.

His hand falls away and I fist my fingers so I don't reach for him. But he offers me his hand when we step off the porch and I take it, allowing myself to take some strength from him.

For several minutes we walk without talking. Up Leighton Ave and down Restix Street until we're walking up the path to another church. This one is Unitarian. It would look like any regular building, a residence, if it wasn't for the peak of the roof and the way it sprawled. It has white siding and a cross on the large gable end.

There is a playground at the side and a large yard with flower beds and benches. Zaiden walks up the path, pulling me with him.

The wooden door is closed, but he pulls it open. As we step inside and the door closes behind me, I feel peace. It's quiet, but not cold.

Zaiden pulls me further inside the lobby and stops at a table where he picks up one of those rubber cause bracelets. This one is a rainbow. There's a cross painted on it in white and the words 'He's Proud of You' on it. Taking my hand, Zaiden stretches it until it sits around my wrist.

"I believe in God," Zaiden says quietly as he pulls me along. There's a man standing off to the side. As he turns and I see his collar, I suddenly feel like I'm intruding on another man's turf. But he smiles at me, welcoming and warm. "But the God I believe in loves everyone equally," he adds as he leads me closer to the priest. "Who you love doesn't matter to Him."

The priest steps forward and offers me his hand.

"This is Ellsworth," Zaiden says, letting my hand go. "Pastor Bob."

Paster Bob smiles kindly. He's young, maybe forties. Early fifties at the most. But he's relaxed, kind, and welcoming. "It's a pleasure to meet you, Ellsworth."

Then he turns to Zaiden and gives him a hug. When he pulls away, he rests his hand along the side of Zaiden's head. "How are you, son?"

Zaiden smiles and nods. "Can we go into the sanctuary for a bit?"

"Of course, Zaiden. Take your time. Let me know if you need anything."

Zaiden nods and takes my hand again, leading me to the double doors. One is propped open and I can see inside. Just like at the cathedral, the ceilings are high and the pulpit is facing us with a large cross behind it, hanging on the wall. There's a dais and a podium.

But instead of an organ, there's a smaller piano. And while the ceiling is high, it's not imposingly unreachable. There are bare wood accents and a modest wooden chandelier with flame-like bulbs. The walls aren't stone but a soothing, welcoming off-white. There are a couple stained-glass windows creating a kaleidoscope of color at the edges of the room, but they're modest and small. Not domineering and almost threatening.

We take a seat toward the front. Zaiden sits close to me, his hand resting on my leg as I lean into his side. My eyes continue to look around as I take in the very different feel of this church than the one I'd committed my life to for the last three years.

"Was your husband Catholic?" Zaiden asks.

I shake my head. "Baptist, I think," I say quietly. "I guess I don't really recall since I never went with him. We didn't get married at a church because I didn't want to. It was our compromise. No church and I'd let him add God into our ceremony." I look at him, bemused. "As long as I was allowed to approve it all. He was fair, and I considered myself being generous since God and faith and all that shit was mentioned at least a dozen times."

My gaze travels to the front before dropping to the bracelet on my wrist. "Honestly, as long as we weren't getting married in a church, I'd have let him write whatever he wanted in the ceremony," I admit quietly.

"Why did you choose Catholic?" he asks.

My hands fist for a minute before he takes the one closest to him and gently pulls my fingers loose. He twists his with mine, and I stare at the way our hands fit. His skin is soft. I swallow.

"I don't know. Because I thought if anyone was going to force me to believe this shit"—I wince as I look around apologetically to no one. That was rude—"that it would be the radical cutthroat bullies."

Zaiden snorts. "That's a strange reasoning and yet, I can completely understand it too."

"I didn't know you went to church," I say.

He shakes his head. "I don't often. Sometimes when I'm feeling a little stressed or sad or something, I'll go. But that's the thing. There's no one right way to be faithful. There's no correct way to pray. I don't have to come here and devote my entire waking, breathing life to proving that I'm a good Christian. I'm honest. I try to be kind. I give to a handful of charities. And I pray on my own."

"And your sexuality doesn't matter," I say.

Zaiden chuckles. "El, I didn't even think about my sexuality until I met you. Even then, I didn't really think about it. I've never truly questioned something that felt right in my life. If I'm filled with a sense of peace and rightness, I just assume that's what I'm supposed to be doing. Where I'm supposed to be going." He squeezes my hand. "Who I should be with."

"God's plan?" I ask, raising a brow and meeting his eyes.

He grins. "I control my destiny. My future. My life. It's *my* plan.

My faith gives me the strength and confidence to achieve it because that translates to faith and confidence in myself."

"He would have liked you," I say quietly, looking at the front of the pulpit again.

"Your husband?" Zaiden asks.

I nod.

We sit in the quiet for a while longer. The burden of grief doesn't feel so heavy right now. Maybe it's because I finally unloaded it for someone to hear. I've been told that acknowledging it is some kind of big step. It might just be the comfortable silence that we're surrounded by. It's not deafening. It doesn't feel like we're being watched and judged. It's just... peaceful.

"Ready to go?" Zaiden asks after we've been there for maybe half an hour.

I nod and we stand. Even looking at the door we came in doesn't feel imposing. Like a threat that if you leave, you're going to be accosted by sinners and attacked by demons intent on challenging your faith.

Instead, it's a welcoming sight. Not so commanding, but open as if it's ready to embrace you.

Is this what it's supposed to feel like? There's no tension or heavy expectations here. No one is lingering in the shadows (I don't even see shadows), ready to pass judgment. There's no confessional for you to admit that you're a shitty human being who's not living your life in a predetermined mold.

Taking a breath, we find Pastor Bob sitting on a couch in the lobby. He stands and joins us as we pause.

"Did you find what you were looking for?" he asks.

I study his face for a minute before nodding. Whatever I was looking for, I don't think I'm leaving without it. I'm not sure what it was, but I feel better.

There's no new institution of faith. I still don't believe that there's a God. But if I were to be convinced somehow, this one seems like a much nicer being. I'd choose this version of God.

"Thank you for letting us in," I say.

He smiles and rests a hand on my upper arm. It's a kind gesture. Meant to be comforting. And I take it as such. Like he's supporting me, a stranger, just because I walked in. "You're welcome here anytime, Ellsworth."

We leave and walk down the sidewalk back toward Zaiden's house. Still hand in hand. It's this simple gesture that makes me feel a little better with each step we take. I'm not alone. I don't have to be alone.

"I'm sorry," I say. Zaiden shakes his head, but I press on. "I should have said something sooner, so you understood why I couldn't... become invested. Why I needed to put boundaries between us. I didn't want to hurt you. I really, really didn't."

"I know."

"If I'd have just told you why I was there—"

"It probably would have convinced me to try harder, Ellsworth." I look at him with a brow raised. He laughs. "You don't believe in God, El. The *only* reason I wasn't pounding down your door a whole hell of a lot more often was because I didn't want to make you choose between me and your faith. One of those things isn't real to you."

I chuckle, looking down at my feet as we walk for a minute.

"What do you want?" Zaiden asks.

"You," I answer without hesitation. His hand tightens around mine. "But I can't give up on his last request, Zay. I can't. Maybe it's misguided and a stretch, but I feel like if I do, then I'm losing him all over again. I didn't really survive it the first time. I may still be alive, but this isn't surviving. It's not living. I'm simply existing without him."

We stop at a corner and I pull Zaiden around so I can finally take him in my arms. "You're the only person who's ever seen *me* since he died," I say, my voice trembling as I try once again to keep my tears in. "I didn't want to feel anymore because it hurts too much. But since the moment you came into my life, I feel again. Sometimes it hurts, but sometimes it's like flying. And I think they're going to be living simultaneously inside me for a while."

Zaiden kisses my neck, pressing his lips to my skin, and takes a deep breath. "There are other ways to keep that promise, Ellsworth. Ways that allow you to be true to yourself, to live your life for you, and still seek God."

I nod, hugging him tighter. I should let him go. We can't just stay out here all day. But I need his hold. His hug is healing something inside me.

"I was clearly a little extreme in the way I decided to throw myself into his request," I say.

Zaiden snorts laughter and pulls away to look at me. "A little? I'm not sure you ever planned to succeed by going that route."

"Maybe I didn't," I admit, resting my forehead on his. "I'm sorry for making this so much harder than it should have been."

"Don't be sorry for how you handled your grief, Ellsworth. Don't ever apologize for that."

Bringing my hands up, I cup the sides of his face so he's forced to meet my eyes. "I love you too," I say and watch as his eyes fill up with tears again. "I've been too afraid to tell you but I do. So fucking much. You breathed life back into me. And you're a fucking amazing man."

He lets out a shaky huff of laughter. "So, what's the plan, El? Where do we go from here?"

That's a good fucking question. The only plan I had coming here was to tell Zaiden the truth. All of it. No matter how many wounds it tore open inside me to bleed for the first time in three years.

I didn't have a plan for after that. But I know one thing—I'm not going to live without this man anymore.

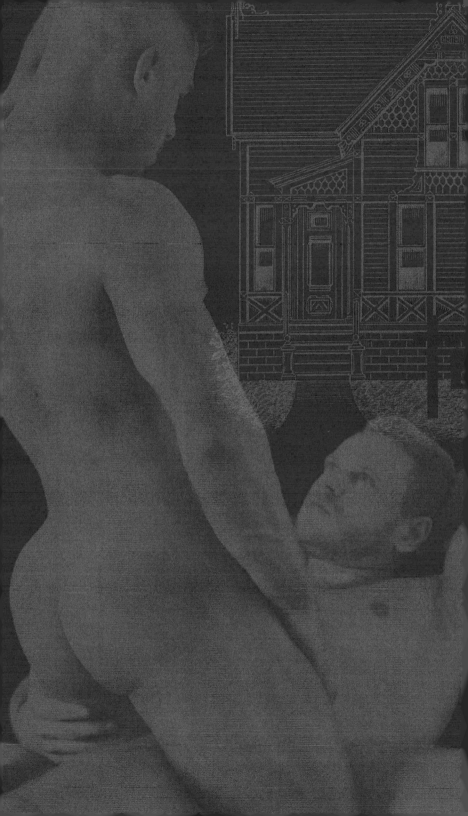

Twelve
ZAIDEN

Six months later

THE SUN IS bright and warm and I stop for a minute outside the cathedral, staring up at the tall and imposing stained-glass window. Enjoying the way the sun reflects off its colors and paints the grassy yard in a rainbow.

Ellsworth's flowerbeds are still beautiful, including the rainbow he planted under the tree by the bench. I sit there for a minute, remembering the day I first saw him here. How my world shifted as soon as I looked into his eyes. Everything in me was just rewritten.

My heart pangs a little remembering those days. While it feels like a lifetime ago, I also remember it like it was yesterday. Every look, every touch. His quiet voice. The way he kissed me and held me and how his voice quaked when he told me he couldn't do this.

As it always does when I remember, my stomach drops and for a second, I have to catch my breath. Nothing has ever hurt quite like that. I admit to having lived a pretty privileged life, so I don't have much trauma or pain to compare it to. But to say I was devastated still feels like the word downplays how I felt.

Taking a breath, I glance at the doors as I stand. There's a priest there, watching me with disapproval. Sometimes I ask them if God would approve of the way they make sure some people aren't welcome in their church. Their look of mortification is only slightly satisfying.

Really, all the radical churches do by instituting things like 'being gay is a sin' and every other bigoted agenda is push their own beliefs down the throats of weak-minded individuals. Those who are desperately looking for forgiveness for whatever it is they've done. These priests are supposed to be the voice of God, spreading His word and sharing His faith.

Not trying to spread hate around the world. There's enough of that out there.

I wave at the priest, who frowns disapprovingly at me. Especially when I pick up my messenger bag that I've replaced the nondescript black shoulder strap with a rainbow one. What can I say? It matches my belt and my sneakers!

And the big flag that's hanging outside the door of the real estate agency. Sam was only all too happy to agree that I hang it. He even hired landscape architects to plant a very blatant rainbow in flowers across the front yard, a nod to Ellsworth's work outside the church.

I turn down the road and follow the sidewalk toward my house. I appreciate that we usually tend to have fair weather. A little rainy sometimes but otherwise, the temperature is generally pretty moderate. In what constitutes as winter, it can get cold at night but the days are usually pretty nice.

My house hasn't changed much except for the addition of the rainbow flower bed out front. While I was ready to put up a flag, I decided I needed to redo the siding first. I am contemplating just using siding as my flag and getting a wide array of colors. I don't want to push it though.

I step inside and set my bag down. The house is quiet. I peek into the bedroom to find it empty, which isn't a surprise. It's usually only occupied at night. The kitchen has a Crock-Pot cooking, and I lift the lid to take a quick look inside. It smells amazing.

Replacing it, I head for the backdoor. It's open and a smile immediately covers my face as I watch Ellsworth outside with the flowers. I lean against the doorframe to watch him.

After his confession six months ago, Ellsworth never returned to the cathedral. He rarely even looks at it when we walk by, which is somewhat regularly since it is located in the middle of downtown. He moved in with me and by that I mean he sleeps here every night. It's not like he had belongings to move, so it was just him.

He hasn't found God yet. But he's attended a service at every church in town and spoken to every priest, pastor, and reverend at each of the churches. I enjoy going with him, just to see how he takes it all in. Seeing him narrow his eyes at something is as adorable as it is when he gives a small, approving smile.

But I can tell, every time we walk out, he hasn't heard or seen anything that makes him believe even a little bit. The bemused smile he sends my way confirms it.

Ellsworth doesn't stop trying, though. He reads religious texts and articles online. We're planning something like a pilgrimage in the following year to a few of the holiest sites to see if he finds his faith there.

What I love most, though, is that he has finally started talking about his husband. I ask about him often but not so much that I make him uncomfortable. I just want Ellsworth to know that he can talk about him. He can remember him. I don't want to take his place. And finally, just a couple weeks ago, Ellsworth started mentioning him sometimes.

Once because he made his husband's favorite meal and he wanted to tell me that. It was just that. Just that 'this was his favorite meal,' but that was enough to have me beaming at him. I didn't comment because I didn't want to push more conversation.

The following day, Ellsworth chose a movie. When it was over, he said, "He loved this stupid movie but for the life of me, I could never see why."

I hugged him tightly to me, and he laughed.

Right now, as I watch him on his hands and knees in the flowers, I know that he's planting his husband's favorite flower. An entire bed of them in all of his favorite colors. I'm hoping he'll let us put a stone or something as an honor to him. But I'll wait to bring that up.

Ellsworth sits back and brushes his hands on his pants, leaving streaks of dirt. He looks around the yard before turning and finding me watching him. He smiles and I know he's not at all surprised to see me there. Nearly every day when I come home, if he doesn't see me right away, I just watch him and think to myself, *this is my life. I have the man of my dreams. Someone I love so damn much it hurts and heals at the same time.*

He gets to his feet and crosses the yard to me. I push off the door and meet him halfway. His mouth immediately covers mine, as it does following every time we're apart for a few hours. Ellsworth holds me loosely for a minute, but then I'm in his arms, his hands under my thighs, and he kisses me deeply.

"Love you," he says into my mouth.

I grin stupidly. "Love you too, El."

His smile is soft as he kisses me lightly. "Have a good day? Sell a house?"

"I closed on two houses and placed an offer," I tell him. "How was your day?"

"I had more flowers delivered," he admits, and glances behind him with a sigh. "But I think I might need to find a job or something."

"Why?"

He shrugs and lets me slide down his body so my feet land on the ground. But his arms are still tightly around me, his forehead on mine. "I don't know. Isn't that part of being an adult? I can't just stay here and plant flowers all day."

"I'd rather you do whatever makes you happy," I tell him. Truth is, I don't spend much time at the office anymore. Since Sam made me a partner, I really don't have to. And though I've never taken advantage of that, since Ellsworth came into my life, I do a little more.

Most days, I go in for two or three hours in the afternoon. Otherwise, I let others take the brunt of the work. The agents we hire.

I can't stand to be away from Ellsworth. He's still too new in my life, and being away from him makes me crazy. Liam says I'm still in the honeymoon phase, but I think this is just what our relationship is. I fall in love with him more every single day. And honestly, I'd rather him stay home and let me take care of him. The thought of him going out for eight or more hours a day to work is not the least bit appealing.

That's not the life I want us to have. I want to spend as much time with him as I possibly can. Every waking minute, when possible. Every second I sleep. And if he's at work for eight hours every day, that severely cuts into our time.

Yeah, I'm a little selfish. I'm not the least bit sorry about it.

Ellsworth sighs. "I have a degree and had a decent paying job once upon a time." He pauses. "There's really no reason that I can't do that again."

"Except then you'll be gone when I get home," I say, pouting a little.

He grins and kisses me, cupping the back of my head and moving me into the position that allows him full access to my mouth. It's deep and consuming. It also makes my dick chub up. But then, all it takes is a look from him and I'm getting hard.

"You'd rather me stay home all day so I'm here when you are than contribute to our household?" he asks quietly.

I'm sure he means it as a joke. Something teasing in which I'm supposed to say 'fine. Get a job.' Joke's on him, though.

"Yes," I say, sucking on his lower lip for a second. Long enough that he growls. "I make more than enough money, El. Let me provide for you."

He sighs, and it sounds a lot like another growl. "We're supposed to be equal in this," he says.

We've never actually talked about our relationship. Not since the day he told me about his husband and that he loves me and wants to be with me. That's as far as that discussion went. It never seemed necessary once he was here with me. And he was still trying to make good on his promise to his husband. I was happy that I could support him while he did that.

"We are," I say, pressing soft kisses to his lips and speaking between them. "That doesn't mean we both need to work. I love that you're here doing something that makes you happy."

"Flowers," he says, amused.

"They bring you peace," I say. "I want you to do whatever you need to keep that peace."

His smile is soft when he brings both hands to cup my face. "You're a really special man, Zaiden Nyles. You know that?"

I shrug. "I'm actually rather selfish. All I want is to spend my time with you and if you go get a job, that's less time that we have together."

His smile grows, and he kisses me again. Deeper this time. It's bordering on filthy, and I can feel his erection pressed firmly to mine now.

Without words, Ellsworth pushes me inside. We don't make it to the bedroom, nor does he even shove the door closed all the way as he pulls my clothes off and I strip him.

You'd think because this is so frequent in any part of the house, we'd have lube stashed everywhere. We don't. So Ellsworth pushes me onto my knees on the couch and shoves his face between my cheeks.

He laps at me, making my breath catch and my heart sprint. I moan loudly and wiggle uncontrollably. His fingers and his tongue take turns, though he's not truly focusing on stretching me. He's more concerned with making me wet.

I think because we started this without much lube, that tends to be the way we have sex. We use his spit more times than not, and I love the rough way it feels. His skin on mine. The excess friction that's not there when we happen to be somewhere that has a tube of lube.

When he moves his body behind me, lining us up and pushing inside, I fall back into his arms and let out a long, low groan. It stings every time. The way he stretches me and makes my ass fit around him is everything. My dick aches at the touch. At the intrusion into my body.

For a minute, he just holds me close once he's balls deep. I swallow, clenching my ass around him to feel every single inch.

"Thank you," he whispers.

I blink slightly, lights flashing before my eyes. "For what?"

"Being you," he says. "Being everything I need. For loving me like you do. For taking care of me when I don't want to take care of myself. For being perfect. For never giving up on me."

Reaching behind me, I lace both my hands in his hair and turn my face so that our lips meet. We kiss as he wraps me tightly in his arms. We're mostly still, with just the slightest rocking of our hips together.

"You're the happily ever after I've been searching for," I tell him. "It was always going to be you and me."

He smiles against my cheek and pulls his hips back slightly before pushing inside me again. I'm still not quiet. Ever. Being with Ellsworth makes me loud in nearly everything I do. Sex aside, my love for him is deafening in the way it screams. My devotion to him is noisy and garish. My obsession with him is lurid and raucous.

Everything about Ellsworth makes me thunderously loud. And in the moments when our bodies are connected, all that noise comes out.

"I love you, Zaiden," he murmurs as he pushes my knees apart further. He leans us forward, still wrapped around me, but now we're resting against the back of the couch, and he has a better angle to drive into me. "You're my only reason life is worth living again. Don't let me fall away."

His words are another confession from him that I know all too well. Ellsworth still struggles when he's having days where he feels particularly guilty for not having made good on his promise. And I know that the only thing keeping him from throwing himself back into the life he hated at the church is me. Loving me.

Logically, he knows differently. But his heart forgets sometimes. Even though he loves me, too. I know he does. I can feel it.

"Never," I promise. I bring one of my hands around to grip his hip as he pushes deeply into me. I fight back the whine about how deep he is in favor of trying to assure him. "You're mine, El. Mine. And I swear to fuck, I will never, ever let you go."

His forehead drops to the back of my neck, and he nods. "I just—"

"I know," I tell him. "But I promise you, your husband would be proud of you, El. So very proud of the man you are."

I feel a tear on my skin and he holds me tighter. So tight that I think he's going to leave a bruise around my ribs. His thrusts aren't quick, but they're hard and deep. It's sensual and intimate.

"Sometimes, I think so," he whispers.

Taking a steadying breath, I push him off me. Ellsworth does as I want and I have him sit on the couch so I can straddle him. We resume our lovemaking, this time in a position where I can kiss him as deeply as he's burying his cock inside me.

"Some promises are hard to keep. Not because you don't want to but because of the very nature of them," I tell him. "You can't force yourself to believe something you don't. You still honor his memory every single day, El." He closes his eyes and I study his face. The lines that form at the corners of his eyes and on his forehead as he processes his grief. "I'm sure he's very proud of you. More so now than when you were in the church."

Ellsworth's eyes open and he's surprised. "Why do you think that?"

"Because that man wasn't you," I tell him gently, kissing his lips. "When he asked you to find God, I am so fucking sure he didn't mean to change who you are entirely. To forget the man you were. Or to give up your entire life and identity to do so. Ellsworth, you're making him more proud of you today than you did for those three years."

He sucks in a breath and closes his eyes again. Then his mouth is on me and he's once again devouring me like he had outside. His focus is back on what we're doing and my orgasm that has been simmering in the back, unnoticed and neglected, suddenly sneaks up on me and I'm crying out in his mouth as I cover both of our stomachs with my cum.

Ellsworth is another couple minutes behind me, but I love the way he growls and grips me punishingly hard as he empties into my ass. The burst of hot, viscous liquid seeping out of my hole around his dick makes me groan.

"I love you," he says, laying us on our sides on the couch. "Till I die, this is where I want to be."

"In my ass," I tease.

I'm relieved when he grins, pressing his lips against mine quickly. "I mean, yes. But in your arms. In your heart. All that sappy shit, Zay. I need you to love me and remind me I'm not a shit husband for not finding God."

"You're so far from a shit husband, El. Even in death, you're honoring him with your entire being."

He nods, and we lay quietly for a minute. Then his eyes open and he looks at me, a soft smile on his lips. "Maybe I shouldn't with my entire being. You deserve more of me."

I shake my head but he stills it with his hand cupping my cheek.

"Yes, you do. Thank you for reminding me that I'm not shit and for letting me mourn and for doing what I need to as I try to find something I don't believe. But Zaiden, my life is now yours. I can't live in the past anymore. You deserve more than that and I'm going to spend every day reminding you that you have my heart."

"Does that mean you'll not get a job?" I ask, trying to lighten the mood because I might cry. Who knew I was such a sappy man?

He chuckles. "Yeah, okay. But if there's ever a time when I need to get a job to take some of the financial burden off you..."

Pressing my lips to his, I smile. "I actually live quite modestly, El. It'll be a very long time before that happens, if it ever happens."

Ellsworth nods. "And... you think that we can..." He bites his lip and studies my face. It's the first time I've seen whatever kind of insecurity he's facing. I kiss him lightly, encouraging him to tell me. "Have a future one day?" he asks.

"We already do, but if you're asking for a wedding and a forever home and a family—however that looks—fuck yes, Ellsworth."

He smiles and hugs me again. "Yes, I want all that. With you. And you can never leave me. You're not allowed to die first."

"Let's not get grim," I say, chuckling. "Let's just focus on the first steps of this future. Wedding first or house?"

"Which do you want?" he asks and I would likely float away if he wasn't holding me so tightly.

"I want to give you both. Which do you want *first*?"

He's quiet as he thinks about it. His sigh is quiet, as is his voice when he answers. "Marry me, Zaiden."

The grin splitting my face is so wide it's painful. "Yes," I tell him. "Fuck yes. Always yes!"

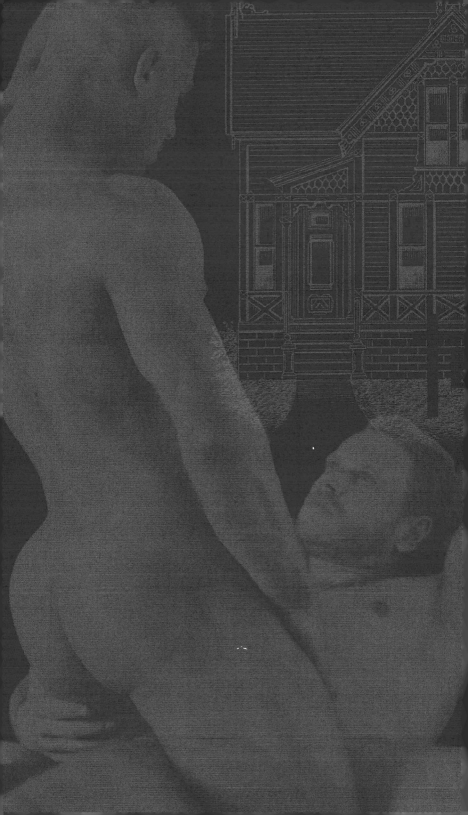

Epilogue
ZAIDEN

1.5 years later

I GREW up thinking I knew exactly what my life was going to be. Being a man, I'd be the stronger person in my relationship. It was my responsibility to care for, protect, and provide for my family. All the heavy lifting. There were expectations placed on me because of my gender.

It's weird to think that all of those expectations are somewhat irrelevant and shatter when you put two people of the same sex together. The same role expectations are on Ellsworth; so then, who takes on the softer role?

What I love perhaps far more than I should is that Ellsworth lets me take care of him. Though it's grudgingly sometimes, he stays home, and lets me bring in the money. He lets me take care of him, physically and emotionally. He lets me make him feel better when he's having a rough day.

This big man lets me hold him as if he were half my size. He trusts me and loves me. It makes me so fucking giddy knowing that.

And then there's the fact that he can pick me up and carry me as if I am half *his* size. There's something liberating about being carried by your partner for no reason except that he can and wants to. Having his hard body against mine is always slightly baffling. I enjoy his hard planes and his features that are completely masculine.

The stubble on his face. His thick cock and heavy balls. The planes of his chest. His deep voice.

I won't even get into the fact that he can fuck me in a way no woman can. There's something visceral and explosive about sex with Ellsworth. It's a drug and I never want to be sober.

Our life isn't perfect. We disagree about things. And we argue from time to time. As the days pass, we find areas where we're very dissimilar, and it can be a challenge to find common ground. But none of that matters. Our love is strong and grows more every day.

Ellsworth hasn't found God and there are days he truly struggles with this. He still feels like he's letting down his late husband by not being able to give him his last request. Personally, I think it's something that he's going to chase for the rest of his life and never find. If his husband knew how much this would tear him apart, I'm sure he wouldn't have asked it of him. Not when he can't relieve him of that stress and pressure when it becomes too much for him.

We've visited every church in the town, attending at least a single sermon. We've also visited several out of town in neighboring cities and villages. Most of the time, he walks out rolling his eyes. But there are times when he looks a bit at peace when we leave too.

In our search for God, we've even visited Jewish temples and Islamic Mosques. And then we've moved away from the Abrahamic religions and have been looking at the more spiritual aspects of religion. He enjoyed the peace that Hindu meditation brought him. And he especially loved the Yule celebration we participated in with a local pagan group. He was especially fascinated when we were allowed to observe a Native American ceremony.

But as much as he loved these things, exploring different cultures and beliefs, he was no closer to believing in something that he just couldn't visibly see with his eyes or feel with his hands. I'm not sure he's a hard-core science minded man, but he can't fathom believing in such a being when the world is such a shit place.

His arguments are valid, and sometimes amusing when he gets all riled up about them.

So, I decided that we are going to go on a trip. For six weeks, we are going to travel the world and visit half a dozen of the most spiritual and holy places in the world.

I planned some US and European stops, then Japan, Cambodia,

and we'd end in Peru. When I presented this to Ellsworth, he just grinned at me like I was God. Like he'd found what he's been looking for. I told him we needed to get him his passport, and he got very quiet.

"They're good for ten years," he said. I nodded, unsure where he was going with this.

And that's how I learned that he didn't actually walk away from his entire life once his husband died. Okay, he did, but he didn't throw it all out. There were now four large boxes stowed in our guest room. For the first few weeks they were there, I'd find Ellsworth standing over them, staring. He didn't open them. Just looked at them.

Until I finally nudged him and said if we need to get a new passport, then we should do that soon. He opened a single box and dug through it until he found said passport. And then he sealed the box again. He shoved them into the closet and shut the door.

I feel good having them with us. The last four pieces of his life before he lost everything. Even if he isn't ready to face them, they'll be there for when he is.

And thus, we spent weeks going to some amazing places. We began in the US, Bahá'í House of Worship in Illinois. It is a large white temple that reminded me of the White House to some degree and includes teachings from all major religions.

We spent a long weekend there while Ellsworth and I sat in on many services. While he enjoyed them and found one in particular to be thought-provoking, he didn't find that it spoke to anything deeper. "They're nice words and a great lesson. But I don't see what this has to do with a higher power," he said.

We left the US to fly west, stopping next in Japan. Kyoto is the Capital of Peace and Calm with some 1,660 Buddhist temples, 400 Shinto shrines, and 60 Christian churches. The city itself was beautiful and calm, but visiting the temples and shrines was something that I wish I'd planned more time for.

As we were leaving, Ellsworth decided if he was going to believe anything, it would be to follow the Buddhist path. "It's not believing in a powerful divinity so much as following a way of life," he told me as we boarded the plane to Cambodia. "I could probably do that. But that's not really what he was asking of me, is it?"

I took his hand, not answering one way or another. If he were alive, I think his husband would tell him it was fine. But I didn't know the man, so I didn't feel comfortable saying as much and it wasn't really my place.

The hike to Angkor Wat was exhausting, but being there and seeing the enormous temple was entirely worth it. I could feel the deep peace and spirituality of the place. For a while, as Ellsworth and I walked around in silence and he took it all in, I thought maybe he found what he was looking for.

We spent well into the evening there before traveling back. As much as I wanted to ask, I didn't. I studied the small smile on his lips and the lightness in the way he walked. But he never spoke of the visit as more than it was one of his favorite places he's ever visited in his life to date.

From Cambodia, we spent a week exploring Stonehenge and Armagh, Ireland where the Celtic pagans had a strong root. Even though Christianity took it over some many hundred years ago, there's Celtic pagan influence and reminders everywhere.

And now we are climbing to our very last stop on this tour. One I am incredibly nervous about because I haven't just planned it as our last spiritual stop, but as a little something more. We're walking with a group and within the group is a Peruvian civil servant.

But first, we need to finish scaling the mountain. It is fucking excruciating. But when we reach the top and set our eyes on Machu Picchu, my heart stops, and I just take in the enormity of it.

"This place unties and resonates all the chakras," Ellsworth reports from the book I handed him on the flight here. I'd given him one like it for every stop we'd made, telling him all about the place we were going. "The main cores of spiritual power in the human body." He pauses as he looks at the pages for a second before looking at me with amusement. "That's my problem, isn't it? My chakras are blocked so I don't have the capacity to believe in any of this."

I chuckle and pull him to my chest. "If that's what you believe, okay."

"What do you think? You've taken me to some epic places, Zay, and I'm still..." He shakes his head. "It's not a waste of time, is it?"

"Any time with you is not a waste of time," I tell him, kissing him lightly. "Seeing how you smile and find peace everywhere we go is not a waste. Watching you smile and laugh and appreciate everything we see and do is definitely not a waste."

His smile is lopsided as I speak. "You're a little sappy today."

I kiss him again. "I love to see you happy. I love to be the one that gives you that happiness. So I'm totally embracing the sappy label today."

Ellsworth chuckles. I follow him around, gently steering him where I want him to go as we slowly make our way to the Sun Temple. There's a single person waiting there and then a few off to the sides.

When we get to the House of the Inca just before it, I pull Ellsworth around to look at me. "Are you happy?"

He grins and nods. "Very."

My palms are a little sweaty and I rub them on my thighs before pulling him close by his hips. He doesn't miss me wipe my hands and looks at me with a brow raised.

"A while ago, we talked about building a future together," I say and Ellsworth immediately smiles. "We listed some milestones, and though you said you wanted them all, I suggested we start with one at a time."

His smile is wide, and he licks his lips. I know what he's expecting at this point. But I don't think the follow up to it will be something he saw coming. Even seeing his smile and being fairly confident he would say yes, I am nearly jittery with nerves.

"I know we've been looking at houses, but I'd really like to get married first. I want to spend my life with you. The moment I laid eyes on you, even if I didn't understand that's what everything in me was saying, I knew it. And though we don't make a habit of talking about the future, maybe we should more than we do, I think we're on the same page."

Ellsworth lays a kiss on my lips. "We are. But hurry up and ask before I do."

Laughing, I lean my forehead against his. "Will you marry me, Ellsworth Sanna? Be my husband and grow old with me?"

He's nodding before the first four words leave my mouth. When I stop, he says breathily, "Yes. Always yes."

"Well... then that only leaves me with one more question." Now he's confused. His brows knit together and he pulls his forehead from mine. "Will you marry me *right now?*"

His eyes go wide. "Now? Here?"

I laugh a little. "Yeah. Right here." I shift and gesture to where the civil servant awaits us at the Sun Temple. He gives us a little wave and Ellsworth stares with his jaw slack. "I might have had an ulterior motive for coming here," I hedge.

For a very long moment during which my heart is ready to beat its way out of my chest, he says nothing. He stares at the man in the temple before looking at me. And then he grins and wraps his arms around my neck.

The relief that rushes out of me makes my knees shake. Fuck, I didn't realize I was ready to pass the fuck out.

"I love you, Zaiden," he whispers. "You have no idea how much."

I hug him tightly and press my face into his neck. "Yes, I do. I love you just as much."

"I didn't think I'd ever feel this way again," he admits. "Hurry up and marry me. I need you to be my husband now."

We don't release each other for another minute, but finally stumble our way up to the civil servant. It's not a particularly sentimental ceremony and there's no God in it. But there is a bit of spirituality. Not so much in the words, but I can feel it all around. Like there's a blessing falling over us. Approval.

When we sign our legal documents, the man leaves us alone and I slip a ring on his finger. The way his eyes glitter in the sun and the smile on his face are things I'll never forget for as long as I live.

"Are you ready for the rest of our lives?" I ask.

Ellsworth cups my cheeks and stares into my eyes. "More than ready, Zay."

"Then I hope you're okay with me extending this trip a bit. I needed to include a honeymoon after our wedding."

Ellsworth laughs and then his mouth is on mine, kissing me deeply and filling me with his love. I wrap my arms around his waist and kiss him back with everything in me.

Author's Note

Thank you for reading. You may see some of these characters again. I love them far too much for this to be a goodbye.

Books by Crea Reitan

MM NOVELS/SERIES

For Puck's Sake

Shiver

Starting Line

Lucky Shot

The Crease (2024)

For Your Love

For Your Time

For Your Heart

For Your Mind

For Your Forever

THE IMMORTAL CODEX

Immortal Stream: Children of the Gods

Mortal Souls

The God of Perfect Radiance

The Hidden God

The God Who Controls Death

Gods of the Dead

Gods of Blood

Gods of Idols

Gods of Fire

Gods of Enoch

Gods of Stone (2024)

INFECTED FAIRY TALES

Wonderland: Chronicles of Blood

Toxic Wonderland

Magical Wonderland

Dying Wonderland

Bloody Wonderland

Wonderland: Chronicles of Madness

The Search for Nonsense

The Queen Trials

Veins of Shade

Finding Time

Neverland: Chronicles of Red

Neverwith

Nevershade

Neverblood

Nevermore

OTHER/STANDALONES

Hellish Ones Novels

Blood of the Devil

House of the Devil

Harem Project Novels

House of Daemon

House of Aves

House of Wyn

House of Igarashi, 1

House of Igarashi, 2

House of Agni

House of Kallan

House of Malak (2024)

Brothers of Eschat

Unsolicited

Equipoise

Paranormal Holiday Novel

12 Days

Satan's Touch Academy

A Lick of Magic

A Touch of Seduction

Fae Lords

Karou

Sweet Omegaverse

Alpha Hunted

Knot Interested

Omegas of Chaingate

Get Pucking Knotty

The Princess and Her Alphaholes Anthology (excerpt of *Wrecked*)

Wrecked

Hell View Manor

Stroking Pride (A Sons of Satan Novel)

A Tale of Steam & Cinders

Terror

Haidee (A Ladies of MC Novel)

About the Author

Crea lives in upstate New York with her dog and husband. She has been writing since grade school, when her second grade teacher had her class keep writing journals. She has a habit of creating secondary, and often time tertiary, characters that take over her stories. When she can't fall asleep at night, she thinks up new scenes for her characters to act out. This, of course, is how most of her meant-to-be-thrown-away characters tend to end up front and center - and utterly swoon-worthy! Don't ask her how many book boyfriends she has...

When not writing, Crea is an avid reader. Her TBR pile is several hundred books high (don't even look at her kindle wish list or the unread books on her tablet). Sometimes, she enjoys crafting; sometimes, exploring nature; sometimes, traveling. Mostly, she enjoys putting her characters on paper and breathing life into them. Oh, and sleeping. Crea *loves* to sleep!

Thank You

I hope you enjoyed Ellsworth and Zaiden's story.

Would you be so kind as to take a moment and leave a review? Reviews play a big role in a book's success and you can help with just a few sentences.

Review on retailer website of choice, Goodreads, and Bookbub

Thank you!!

Crea Reitan

PS - If you find any errors, spelling or the like, please do not use your ereader to mark them. The algorithms pull the book! Instead, please reach out to me on Facebook at https://www.facebook.com/Crea.Reitan or via email at LadyCreaAuthor@gmail.com. Thank you!!

Printed in Poland
by Amazon Fulfillment
Poland Sp. z o.o., Wrocław